FRIDAY NIGHT IS FISH SUPPER NIGHT

About the author

I was born in Exeter, Devon in 1972, and from an early age I discovered I had an overwhelming desire and passion to creating something. Whether it be a colourful abstract painting, a fine ink illustration or a piece of poetry, the overriding passion, mixed with my imagination and energetic attitude was to try and express myself creatively.

In February of 2019 I completed my first children's story – *The Spiky & Spiny Night Time Adventures of Nikky & Flick.*

After that story was accepted for publication, I felt that the next most natural progression for me would involve trying to create a longer piece of work. So, *Friday Night is Fish Supper Night* is my debut teen fictio

This story reflects on a number of issues that I myself have faced and confronted over a twenty-five-year period. So, to finally feel able to write such a relevant, partly personal story of past, and to some degree present feelings and emotions has for me been a very cathartic experience.

Cass Stoddart

FRIDAY NIGHT IS FISH SUPPER NIGHT

Vanguard Press

VANGUARD PAPERBACK

© Copyright 2020
Cass Stoddart

The right of Cass Stoddart to be identified as author of
this work has been asserted by him in accordance with the
Copyright, Designs and Patents Act 1988.

A CIP catalogue record for this title is
available from the British Library.

ISBN 978 1 78465 746 8

*Vanguard Press is an imprint of
Pegasus Elliot MacKenzie Publishers Ltd.*
www.pegasuspublishers.com

First Published in 2020

**Vanguard Press
Sheraton House Castle Park
Cambridge England**

Printed & Bound in Great Britain

Dedication

To Keith and Lynda Bowden, for their continued encouragement, support and love.

TRIGGER WARNING

The themes explored in this book include suicide and self-harming.

For help with these and any other mental health issues, please visit mind.org,uk for information and support.

Chapter 1

"It's Friday, Franny," shouts Tom, "fish supper night, treat night, from Fat Eddie's; finger fat chips and chunky, crispy, battered cod."

"I know," comes my slightly irritated and rushed reply; to be honest, I can't focus on our Friday night, vinegar-dowsed treat. My mind is firmly focused on today's swim meet against Okement Grove, our nearby private school rivals.

"Franny, have you decided what you are eating tonight?" Tom shouts excitedly.

"No!" I reply. "I can't think about that now, Tom. Have you brushed your teeth and got your school uniform on?"

"Yes! You ask me that every morning."

"Well, if I didn't, you would never get yourself ready."

Tom is bouncing around in his bedroom, obviously excited, it is Friday, last day of school, and treat night too. Pip, our younger sister, is less excited, she is still in her *SpongeBob SquarePants* pyjamas, and half asleep. She yawns then rubs her big blue saucer-sized eyes.

"*SpongeBob Adventures, SpongeBob Adventures*," she calls out. The DVD is an old Christmas present; I am surprised it still works after being played day in and day out; so, Pip's first thoughts are always a choice between *SpongeBob* or *The Smurfs* movie, another old favourite. I've never really understood why these blue-bodied, white-floppy-hat-wearing dwarfs get so excited and seem so surreally happy about working in a cheese factory. Anyway, it is *SpongeBob* this morning, it's her favourite, so I push play and begin bowling up breakfast.

"Coco Rice, or Sugar Puffs?" I call out as I do every morning. "Sugar *Huffs*," replies Pip; "Chocolate Rice," comes Tom's loud reply.

I stick to my browning banana for brekky; Dad says it's good for energy, stored energy, ideal for swimmers.

As I put the milk back, I see Dad's note, a yellow Post-It note stuck to the fridge door. *Hi all its Friday, have a great swim Fran, Tom, stop thinking about Fat Eddie's! And give Pip a Kiss from me, luv u all dad xx*

Our dad, Frankie, or "Frankie Doors" as everyone else calls him, always leaves a little note. Dad is up and out the door by five-thirty. He works for the local council as a bin man. Dad keeps his work clothes by the front door along with his worn-out steel-toecap boots. I wish Dad would keep his work stuff near our *back* door because every time I grab our coats I can smell a cat pee whiff. Dad says it comes from the rubbish bags he handles every day.

Tom is shovelling Coco Rice into his mouth, and Pip seems to be feeding the carpet her "Sugar Huffs," as she calls them, when the door knocker knocks.

"Come in, Aunty Pam," I shout out. Aunty Pam comes wobbling in, holding her plastic green Harrod's bag, which she makes a point of showing off at any opportunity. I am not sure why, you can hardly make out the worn gold lettering, she must have had it for years, or even got it in a charity shop.

"Is Pip ready?" asks Aunty Pam.

"Not quite, she's just finishing her cereal, Aunty."

"What! She's not even dressed. How am I to cope, Franny?" Tom sniggers into his last spoonful of chocolatey milk.

"Don't worry, Aunty Pam; I will put Pip's clothes out on her bed for you after I finish my breakfast. Me and Tom are running a bit late so must head off to school soon. Tom, go grab your bag, I'll tidy up here and sort Pip's clothes out."

I choose the most awkward, fiddly-buttoned outfit for Pip and lay it out on her bed ready for Aunty Pam.

I grab my school bag and sling my canvas gym bag over my shoulder. I call Tom over, then zip up his grubby blue parka. Tom and I turn and blow Pip a kiss goodbye. "See you, Aunty Pam," I say. "See you, Pam," Tom murmurs, and we head out. The early summer sun strikes my face as I firmly shut the front door behind us.

Tom and I take a familiar route towards our schools. Tom is in his last year of primary school and is eleven. I am nearly fifteen, with one year of comp to go.

We turn right at the bottom of our street, Oak View, and then head up towards Pine Rise where we usually meet up with my best friend Tanya Sykes and her oddly quiet, jet-black curly-haired younger brother, Bobby. We get to the junction of Pine Rise and Maple Drive when I spot Tanya and Bobby on the other side of the road.

Tanya is looking great, as she always seems to. She has naturally blonde curls and big, bright blue eyes; Bobby on the other hand has dark almost wire-like hair, with wispy, unkempt chin hairs and thin, black sideburns. I do wonder sometimes if they are actually related.

We head along Maple Drive now, with Tanya and me doing all the talking. We turn right into Fore Street, past the infamous Eddie's, which is next door to the originally named Porky the

Butcher's. Opposite that is the Fountain Inn, the only pub in our small town of Tawton.

My dad says, "A night out in the Fountain is like a prison sentence; bad food, no atmosphere and little or no intellectual conversation."

Tom, who earlier couldn't stop talking and jumping around, had become quiet and now is walking to my left, as far away from Tanya Sykes as the pavement allows. I noticed Tom's change in behaviour a few weeks ago when Tanya had asked, "Have you had a haircut, Tom?" Tom stumbled, almost stuttered his reply, "No, no, just started using a bit of gel," he replied. "Oh! Looks nice, Tom," Tanya had said. Since then Tom is a quiet and well-behaved pleasure to walk with once we meet up with Tanya and Bobby.

We turn left now into Leaf Lane, ahead is Tawton Primary. Tom sprints off without a goodbye or a see-you-later. Tanya, aware of her effect on Tom, blows him a kiss, "See you later, Tommy," she shouts.

Tom leaves us behind; blushing, I bet! Then Tanya, me and the curly, wispy haired Bobby head up towards Tawton High, our comprehensive school, which is in the same grounds as Tom's primary, but separated by a fierce-looking chained link fence.

As we get closer to our school's entrance, Tanya spots Teddy Newcombe. Teddy is in our year, and Tanya has a major crush!

Tanya has mentioned once or twice, or maybe twenty times, the day Teddy and she first met. Tanya was sent to see the headmaster, Mr Harding, for over-application of makeup. Teddy was already waiting outside Mr Harding's office for a Bunsen burner misuse charge! So, there they were, Bonnie and Clyde, awaiting their judgement.

Nervously, Teddy had broken the ice by asking, "What you here for?"

Tanya giggled, blushed and then explained that Miss Womack didn't approve of her cherry red lipstick and over-application of fake tan. Well, sparks sparked, and internal fires were lit, Teddy was called in, and Tanya was in love.

My morning lessons of English, chemistry and "I-haven't-got-a-clue-maths" pass without any major incident. Well, there was a chalk thrown, voices raised, detention threatened moment by Mr Humphreys in maths, but that was just a Geoffrey Merve episode. We all have become familiar with Geoffrey Merve and his disruptive manoeuvres, he just can't sit still, and shouts random swear words every few minutes. Especially in maths.

I think he must be unhinged, but my classmates say he is just "a bit special." He lives at Fairview, a caravan site, situated just outside Tawton on a purpose-built traveller's site. Geoffrey has a younger sister, Stacey Merve. Stacey is a first year, she has a temper, and many of the older kids, like myself, give Stacey a wide berth. She is all ginger curls and big freckles; no one messes with Stacey Merve.

The end of lesson bell rings; thank God, no more maths for a few days. I have arranged to meet Tanya outside our canteen so we could have lunch together, as we always do, but to be honest, I am becoming quite nervous now, my stomach is churning, and for the first time today my mum enters my thoughts.

Our swim meet is only an hour or so away, so I don't eat the spaghetti Bolognese with grated cheese or the curled-up, cardboard-brown chips that are on offer today.

Tanya has just started devouring her cheesy chips and starts sipping noisily on her second can of coke, when I notice Tanya's younger brother Bobby. He is actually speaking to another human being, I think at first, but then I quickly realise that Bobby is just pointing and gesticulating towards an extra-large portion of spaghetti Bolognese.

I nick the last, sad-looking cheesy-covered chip off Tanya's plate. Maybe that will settle my stomach.

Lunch finished, well, one chip and a swig of Tanya's Coke; so, Tanya and I head off towards our pool, which is in a separate block to our main school and next to our sloping sports fields.

Our swimming pool is a worn-out, murky-green relic, unlike Okement's pristine, hospital-smelling, brand-new and ice-white facility; the tiles in our pool are off-blue in colour, delightfully speckled in mouldy vintage black.

Our changing rooms; well, at first you see our worn-out wooden benches, which are covered with Tipp-Ex style graffiti, and then you look up towards our un-lockable, bent, metal lockers. If you are lucky, you get a clothes hook, but there are only three, so you must get to the changing rooms early. Me and Tanya are always early, always first through those heavy wooden changing room doors.

***

Aunty Pam has fumbled, buttoned and cursed her way through Pip's morning outfit. "Come on then, Pip, shall we take a walk down to the town? I need a wholemeal loaf and some non-fat milk. We could pop into Eddie's, a cappuccino will be welcomed, and we could get you one of those Fruit Shoots things you love. Sound good, my lovely?" Pip nods her head in approval.

Pip, who is only three, is snug and warm in her outfit, and is definitely missing the end of

SpongeBob SquarePants and his bizarre, quirky, underwear-related adventures.

"Come on then, lovely. We will take a wander into town; sun's coming out," says Aunty Pam.

Aunty Pam buttons up Pip's pink, fluffy-hooded coat and then twitches her nose, "What's that smell, Pip? It smells like wee. You haven't had a wee have you, love?" Pip moves her head from side to side and begins to clamber into her bright red pushchair.

Aunty Pam, who is my mum's older sister, lives just ten minutes away in Poplar Grove. She lives in a fairly new semi-detached house that always seems to smell of soup. She is divorced; her ex-husband Gerald ran off with Janice Holder. Janice used to work with my mum in our local Spar shop.

Janice, by all accounts, would meet Gerald over her dinner hour; they would sometimes meet at Aunty Pam's or take a car journey up to the nearby moor. Janice had been seeing Gerald for nearly a year before Aunty Pam unexpectedly came home early from her bingo session and found Gerald and Janice... well, on the floor!

So, Aunty Pam lives alone now, apart from her cats, Fluffy and Spot.

Fluffy is fine, you never really get to see her, but Spot, well, he always seems to be on edge somehow, always happy to be stroked but never seems completely relaxed. He wags his tail, then shows his claws when you stop. I stay away from Spot, and make sure Pip does too. Tom never seems to have any problems with Spot. Maybe it's a boy thing.

My Aunty Pam takes care of Pip, she has done since my mum, Launa, was committed to Park Place, just over five months ago now.

Aunty Pam is a large lady who has a beachball round belly, a short, manly haircut and a thick neck. She looks after Pip until my dad finishes work, which is normally around three o'clock. Pip will be heading off to pre-school soon, so Aunty Pam can get back to her sewing and decoupage; whatever that is!

I know my dad really appreciates Pam's help, but I think truthfully, Dad is looking forward to having Pip playing and mixing with other SpongeBob and Smurf converts.

***

Tanya and I push the heavy, squeaky wooden changing room doors wide open. "We are here," shouts Tanya, as if a large crowd of people are awaiting our arrival. We are there first, of course. We hang our bags up next to each other, as we always do. Tanya, who is now sitting down upon our graffiti-adorned benches, starts to stretch her legs and point her toes; I instinctively start rotating my arms and moving my head from side to side.

Once again, my mum comes into my thoughts; she is always there really, but especially so when I am up for a swim meet, or sitting an exam, I guess. My mum enters my thoughts when I am at my most competitive, scared, or nervous.

She was once herself a keen competitive swimmer. I have her junior gold winning medals hanging proudly in a mahogany and glass frame on my bedroom wall. She swam for county at junior level, and even had trials with the GB junior swimming squad.

I wish my mum could be here and watch me today, but I know that after her mental breakdown she can hardly deal with our once-weekly visits, let alone be out among people and sounds she doesn't know.

My dad, who I think really holds it all together, seems to be positive, suggesting and trying to convince us all that Mum will get better and be home soon. "She will be bugging you, Tom, about your messy bedroom and Xbox overuse, and making sure you, Fran, are training every day and eating your pasta and bananas! And Pip, well, Mum will just tickle and hug you until you burst, I think."

I enjoy it when Dad plays and jokes like that. It makes me smile; it feels good to imagine Mum being home again.

I think Tom struggles the most, he and Mum are so very close, I still feel that he, like me, doesn't really understand what is going on. Tom seems to dismiss Mum's illness, putting it down to "stress", a word he has heard from Aunty Pam. Stress is part of it I am sure, but seeing Mum, really seeing her, unable to talk, unable to smile or even force a laugh; that image haunts me; that painful image is felt deep in the pit of my stomach; it always makes me feel numb and peculiar.

Tanya is pulling, tugging and adjusting her jet-black swimsuit. "Does it look good, Fran?" she asks.

"Yes, Tanya, it looks great." Honestly! *Think about the swim,* I think to myself.

Tanya is our school's best swimmer. Last year she was the only winner against Okement Grove. Tanya, like me, swims the 50m freestyle and is in our 4x50m freestyle team.

Last year, at Okement Grove, in their Olympic-sized, pristine-clean pool, Tanya had finished first, well in front of Okement's best, Verity Brown. I struggled and huffed and puffed my way to third.

Our other sprint swimmer, Clare Brook, was still swimming when Tanya was slipping on her tracksuit bottoms.

I was sort of happy with third, but thought at the time: Next meet, next time, I am going to win; I am going to demolish all of them, even Tanya.

"Morning Eddie, lovely sunny day, isn't it?"

"Hi, Pam, hello, little Pip, yes a glorious day," replies Eddie.

"A small cappuccino and a blackberry Fruit Shoot, to drink in please, Eddie."

Aunty Pam has already made her daily visit to Spar, our one and only shop, she's brought her daily loaf, a pint of non-fat milk and a Kinder egg for Pip; Aunty Pam has proudly put her buys into her green Harrod's bag.

"Let's take a seat by the window, Pip, we can watch the world go by."

Aunty Pam is a regular at Eddie's; Eddie's is a cafe during the day, and then at night, Eddie serves up his infamous fat chips, huge portions of crispy battered cod, with a choice of two homemade flavours of curry sauce.

Aunty Pam loves to shop. She's always making excuses to visit the Spar; I think she has taken a fancy to Malcolm Downs. Malcolm is the shop manager and always spares a minute or two for Aunty Pam.

"One small cappuccino with complimentary biscuit, and one blackberry Fruit Shoot with complimentary lollipop; enjoy!" Eddie says.

"I see Frankie Doors later? Three fat chips, three cod, one battered sausage and two curry sauce, is it?"

"I guess so, Eddie, it is Friday so Frankie will be in I am sure."

***

Tanya is now stretching her legs, and tweeting and updating her Facebook page one-handed. Our changing room is filling up now. Miss Baxter, our swim coach, is patrolling up and down inspecting our warm-ups "Put that phone away, Tanya, I want us all to concentrate on today's swim please." Tanya always seems to be calm and collected before a swim, while I get awful nerves and become full of self-doubt.

"We did well last year," Miss Baxter says, "but today we will do better. Tanya, I expect a fast time from you today, and Fran, remember your stroke sequence and breathing, I expect you to push Tanya all the way."

I take my time warming up, I always do; I have a routine, taught to me by my mum. Before I put my swimsuit on, I start to slowly rotate my head, then shoulders, working every major muscle group, all the way down to my toes. I do this routine three or four times, until my nerves ease off a little.

I am in my swimsuit now, brand new thanks to Dad, my old suit was frayed, worn out, almost see-through, so when I asked Dad for a new swimsuit, he replied positively, like he always seems to do.

That night we looked online and found a great deal on swimsuits and two days later a small, brown jiffy bag was posted through our letter box. A brand new, jet-black Speedo swimsuit. It fitted perfectly. *I feel good, I look good,* I thought as I tried it on, and admired the fit in my bedroom mirror. Black is the colour for me.

Miss Baxter tells us that Okement have arrived, and we should keep warm and put our tracksuits on. I imagine them stepping off their shiny new bus, all dressed in the same school colours, green and gold pristine tracksuits with brilliant white trainers. I laugh to myself, the thought of their first sight of our changing rooms, I imagine them being more disgusted by the spelling of the graffiti than the actual mess of the Tipp-Ex splattered words.

***

Tanya has her headphones on, she's tapping her fingers on her right leg, and holding her iPhone in the other hand. I rest my head on my chest, everything is quiet, I don't want to, but when things are this quiet, I can't help it, I begin to think about that day, the day I found my mum: Monday the 13th of January 2018.

My day had started with a familiarity I am sure exists in many homes: the queue to use the bathroom, the what's-for-breakfast, the normal morning chit-chat, with the TV noise on in the background.

Tom and Pip didn't notice, I am sure, but I did; Mum was still in her clothes from the night before. I only really realised it when I noticed a food stain on her white blouse from our tea from the previous night. My mum is so particular about her appearance that the stain stood out; it stood out as an unfamiliar sight, on what seemed to be just another normal start to our day.

"You okay, Mum?" I asked.

"Yes, luv, just feeling really tired, I didn't get much sleep last night."

"Mum, you remember I am going to the park with Noah after school today?"

"Yes, Tom, you have a good time, just make sure you are home by six, okay?"

"Will do, Mum. What's for tea later?"

"Oh God, Tom! I can't think about that. Honestly, is your stomach the only thing you can think about? There are bigger things to worry about, you know!"

Mum rarely raised her voice at Tom, especially over a question that Tom seemed to ask every morning over breakfast. I felt uncomfortable but didn't understand why. Breakfast was eaten in a strained kind of silence. Mum didn't eat her toast and only took a sip of her coffee before heading, without saying a word, into the front room. Tom and I grabbed our school bags and kissed Pip a goodbye on her head.

"Remember, Fran, your Aunty Pam is looking after Pip today as I am working a double shift in the shop, so can you sort some tea out; there is a lasagne defrosting in the fridge, just read the instructions, and maybe make a salad."

"No problem; what's Dad up to?"

"God, Fran! I told you last night, your dad's working overtime. Again. He won't be home until half-six at the earliest."

"All right, Mum, I was only asking." Something is wrong, I remember thinking, everything seemed strained, tense and uncomfortable, my stomach felt sick.

Tom and I headed out the door, we both said our goodbyes, but Mum never replied. Just another school day, I thought, but a day that I would forever relive in my mind. I remember at dinner time that day, sharing my chips with Tanya, and she had asked if I was okay.

"Not sure; my mum seems stressed. She even raised her voice to Tom this morning."

"Fran, my mum's like that all the time, she's always shouting at Bobby, and telling me off."

"Not like this, Tanya. My mum seems different, detached, not herself somehow."

I remember in my final lesson, geography, wishing it would just end; it seemed to go on and on, my stomach seemed taut and sick-filled, and my chest started to feel tight. The lesson bell rang, and I remember rushing out of the classroom, hitting tables as I went. "Fran, where you going? What's the rush?" asked Tanya as I sprinted out of the school gates.

To this day I can't explain the feeling I was having, I just needed to get home, I had tears in my eyes. I ran, I ran fast, faster than I thought I could ever run, I remember my school bag was bouncing annoyingly on my back as I sprinted along Fore Street.

I turned left onto our street, sweat was dripping down my back, and my legs were burning. I reached our front door and gave it a push, it opened. Our front door being unlocked only heightened my senses, and fears. "Mum… Mum," I called out. I didn't expect a response, Mum should have been at work. Suddenly, as I turned into our front room I saw Mum, lying flat out on the sofa. I dropped to my knees, my stomach in my mouth; I could tell by her posture that she wasn't just asleep, her face looked grey, her arms seemed contorted, bent unnaturally over her chest, her legs were straight and stiff-looking, and resting on the sofa arm.

"Mum… Mum!" I didn't know what to do. I grabbed Mum's head and held it to mine. I looked down and saw pills, a few white, oval, small pills spread out on our front room's wooden floorboards.

It seemed like an age before I rested Mum's head down and rushed towards the phone, which is hanging in the kitchen. "Dad, Dad, it's Mum... Mum; she's asleep, I can't wake her." To this day I can't really remember why I didn't mention the pills. "What? What are you talking about, Fran?"

"It's Mum, she doesn't look normal, she, she looks dead, Dad!

"Just breathe, Fran; I am on my way, I am leaving right now."

I remember the waiting, I remember thinking about watching TV upstairs, brushing my teeth, or even having a shower. *God, has Dad rung for an ambulance?* I thought. After about five minutes, I went back downstairs, slowly tiptoeing my way down; I don't know why, but it felt like the right thing to do. I nervously went into the front room; Mum was in the exact same position as when I had left her. I couldn't face spending more than a minute or so by Mum's side, I could hear a soft breathing sound, but it wasn't consistent, so I held my own breath as I tried to listen to Mum's distant and irregular breathing. I held her hand, but it was cold to the touch, so I placed it back down onto her chest. *God, where is Dad, I need help.* I stepped away from Mum and glanced out the window; *no sign of anybody.* As I looked back at Mum and her ghostly white face and strange body posture, she looked to me like she was dying. I couldn't stay in that room anymore, so I quietly made my way back upstairs, unsure of what to do, or how to feel.

I heard the sirens first, then the sound of our front door being loudly pushed opened. A few seconds later another sound, a sound I'll never be able to forget, it was a cry, a wailing, painful cry, then a scream from somewhere deep and dark, the noise, more animal like than human.

"Launa… Launa, what have you done? Oh God, no! Wake up, Launa, you've got to wake up!"

"Mr Goode, let us see to your wife, please, Mr Goode, we've got it from here."

"Fran, where are you?" I could hear my dad scrambling up the stairs, I pictured him on all fours, as he frantically made his way up to me. "Fran, where are you? Where are you, love?" I saw the flashing blue lights reflecting their warning glare onto my white bedroom walls.

My dad rushed into my bedroom, he was breathing heavily, and I remember thinking that he looked smaller somehow, he seemed gaunt; his face was white, and his eyes were black and full of fear.

"Oh, Fran, Fran my love, Mum's going to be okay. I am going to make it better. Oh God, Fran, why?" Dad fell to his knees and held me tight as I sat on the edge of my bed.

We both cried uncontrollably and tightened our hold of each other, I didn't want to let go of him and felt like I never could. "Fran, just wait in your room, love, I'm only going to be downstairs, but I've got to be with your mum now."

I stayed in my room, just staring blankly out of the window, I lost all sense of time, I could hear the unfamiliar speech of the ambulance crew, and then heard my dad's voice. I never actually heard what they were saying, but I felt numb, useless, paralyzed from head to toe; Tom and Pip filled my confused thoughts.

Dad soon came into my room again, tears in his eyes.

"Fran, I'm going in the ambulance with Mum, I know it's hard, but I need you to stay here and wait for Tom. Aunty Pam is on her way with Pip, and she'll stay with you all until I get home, okay?

"Of course, Dad," I replied, but I felt so confused and upset, I just wanted to be with Mum.

It felt like an age before Tom got home from the park, he could tell I was upset and asked where Mum was. I didn't really lie, but I told him Mum was feeling ill, and Dad had taken her to the hospital. Tom looked concerned, but I was surprised by how calm he seemed at first, then as the minutes slowly passed by, Tom found his voice and kept asking all sorts of questions. Questions I couldn't and wouldn't answer; I felt the need to protect him from the truth, so I explained that I had found Mum at home, and that she said she was exhausted, and felt weak and faint.

I also told Tom that Dad had come home early after Mum had called him at work, and that Dad had then decided to take Mum to A & E in Okement just to be on the safe side.

Again, Tom looked concerned, but his questioning stopped. I stayed in the front room with Tom and Pip and pretended to be interested in the game Tom had started to play. Later on, Aunty Pam was stirring some soup and keeping her eye on the oven and its browning garlic bread, when her phone rang.

"Oh, Frankie, I don't know what to say, how is she doing now?"

I watched Aunty Pam as she talked to Dad, her mouth hardly moved, but I could tell by her expression that things at the hospital weren't going great; *This is so very wrong*, I thought. She only spoke for a minute or two, and I noticed that she wiped a tear from her eye as she put her phone down.

"Kids, that was your dad, your mum's doing okay, she's asleep and resting right now. He's going to call again in a bit, all right?"

Tom was playing frantically on his Xbox, and Pip, who was propped up by a pillow, was watching Tom storm an enemy stronghold. Tom just nodded his head and glanced towards Aunty Pam. I got up and ran upstairs, screaming inside, I reached my bedroom, fell flat onto my bed, and started crying uncontrollably. I stayed hidden in my room for what seemed like hours.

I felt numb, peculiar, my emotions were everywhere back then, I even felt embarrassed for a few weeks. *What would people say, what would they think?* And now, it seems that I just constantly worry about how my mum's suicide attempt will affect others; what the hell is that all about?

All I know is that I don't ever want to feel like that again.

Chapter 2

Tanya and I are called towards our lanes for the 50m freestyle race. I feel ready, my warm-up has gone well, and somewhere in my being I see myself winning.

Tanya is in lane two, next to Verity Brown in lane one and I am in lane three, a good lane, right in the middle of the pool. To my right is Okement's Bella Goode; she is a strong swimmer but goes out too fast, I remember that from last year. My swim stroke sequence and practiced breathing enters my thoughts.

I take my starting stance and wait, a painful wait for the starting gun. My dive and forward stroke are strong, my leg kick is clean. I rise, as planned, on my second stroke, cutting through the water, crisp and true. My stroke sequence kicks in; I power forward taking strong purposeful breaths.

I head home, pushing forward from the turn, muscles burning; but arms stretching forward, legs kicking hard, my position unknown. I surge forward, hearing distorted spectator cheers. I hit home hard, striking the wall in a powerful stroke; I think my swim's gone well, I could have won.

I remove my swimming goggles and take short shallow breaths, my whole body is aching; to my left Bella is still in her goggles, to my right Tanya has her goggles resting on her head, she's looking down towards the light blue choppy water. The girls to my left are just finishing their swim.

I feel a touch on my shoulder and look up. The judge says, "Well done, Fran, you've won."

"Yes!... Are you sure?" I say. Miss Baxter, joining the judge at the poolside, agrees excitedly. "Definitely; lane three by a mile." I let out a high-pitched yelp and punch the water.

A happiness surges all over me, my first thought is that my mum will be so proud of me, my dad will smile, a large, knowing smile we both share. Tom will want to celebrate and will suggest we buy a cake. Pip will tap my head and stroke my hair; I love it when Pip does that.

The 4x50m freestyle passes quickly, and to be honest, without my full concentration; I swim well, but after only 75m we are a long way behind.

"Did you not try, Fran? Honestly, I would have thought you of all people would have tried harder." Tanya is sore after losing the individual sprint. *Bitch!* I think; how dare she question my commitment.

***

Frankie comes through the front door after his shift and kicks off his work boots by the front door.

"Hi, Pam. How's my baby? Where's my little Orange-Pip?"

"She's having a nap, Frankie, she's been full of it, I've never known such a fidgety young girl, she doesn't say much, but she can't sit still, can she? And Fran's choice of outfit today was really unhelpful. We had a nice day though. I took her to Eddie's, then we had an hour at the park, she loves those swings, she insisted on going higher and higher; I'm worn out."

"Sounds good, Pam. Franny and Tom will be home soon. God, I hope Fran's swim went well.

"Pam, are you coming tomorrow?"

"Not tomorrow, Frankie; I thought I would visit Launa on Sunday. I'm going to take her out for a walk, down along the Riverbank; Frew's Slope, you know it? I may even make a little picnic."

"Lovely spot, Launa will enjoy that."

Pam grabs her bag and gently touches Frankie on his broad shoulders. "She's getting there, love, you will see; she will be well enough to come home soon."

"I hope so, Pam, the kids are missing her like crazy. Anyway, see you over the weekend, and thanks Pam, as always; thanks for your help."

"My pleasure, love, anytime, you know that."

***

Tanya and I don't really speak until I break the uncomfortable silence and ask if I can use her shampoo, "Come on, Tan, be happy for me."

"I am, Fran, really I am, sorry for being such a bitch."

I feel glad that me and Tanya are talking again but can't help feeling disappointed and a little let down by my best mate's attitude. I take a shower and try to wash off that chlorine chemical smell.

"You going straight home, Fran?"

"Yes, I am going to meet my brother and head home to show Dad my winner's medal; he will be itching to hear."

"Why don't you just ring him?"

"No, no, I want to see his reaction when I tell him."

"Okay, text me over the weekend then."

"Will do."

I quickly slip into my tracksuit and put my scuffed, white trainers on. I can't wait to tell Dad, Tom and Pip my news and show off my first ever winner's medal.

I run; I sprint fast towards Tom's school gates. Tom comes out ten minutes before me usually but today, as planned, he is waiting, waiting with his best mate, Noah.

Tom is slouched over the black metal railings outside his school's entrance. He has a broad cheeky grin on his face, "Franny! Fran, you won! Mr Potts told me in last lesson; we should get a cake to celebrate."

Noah grunts his approval on my win and Tom ruffles my still damp, long, dark hair, "Well done Fran, Dad's going to be so happy."

Tom, Noah and I walk happily down Fore Street, chatting and joking; Tom is skipping, Noah is trying to trip Tom up; we are all pleased and happy it's Friday. Noah heads off to the right at the bottom of Fore Street. "See you tomorrow, Tom; four o'clock at the park?"

"Yes, I'll be there. Bring your new *Call of Duty* for a borrow, bro."

Tom unusually takes hold of my hand. "Fran, Mum's going to be so proud of you." I well up, tears sting my already chlorine-stained red eyes; this is the first time Tom has spoken to me like this.

"Oh, Tom, thanks, I just want Mum better, and at home too."

We both wipe away our tears and head towards home, towards Dad and Pip, and that warm, secure familiar Friday feeling.

Dad is sitting and smoking a roll-up on our front doorstep, the front door is wide open so he can hear if Pip wakes up.

"Hey, how goes it, Tommy the thumb and double-dare Fran?"

"I won, Dad; I won, my first gold ever!"

My dad leaps up, he slings his fag to the floor and then literally lifts me up towards the sky. "Oh, my darling, you star, you are a star." My dad can't hold back his own tears, "Bloody hell, Fran, that's fantastic."

Tom is jumping up and down, "Let's get a cake, let's get a cake."

"A cake!? Let's get two!" Dad shouts.

I have never felt so light, so free, my body is alive and my thoughts full of positive, possible futures. I can tell my dad feels alive too, he finds it hard to show emotions usually but now is bouncing around kicking Tom's football in the front garden; "Goooaaallll," he shouts out.

"Good kick, Dad," Tom says.

I hear Pip's familiar cry and head up the stairs, "Hello, beautiful, how are you my little Orange-Pip?" Pip wipes her eyes and then points towards her teddies. I grab her favourite, a small soft *SpongeBob SquarePants* teddy. I smother her belly, then tickle Pip with it.

"Goal," Tom shouts. Pip and I head out to the front garden, Dad is in goal and Tom is dribbling his football. Pip and I take a seat on our doorstep and watch a happy, sun-soaked family scene.

Dad collapses to the floor as if he had been shot down by a far-off sniper. "Let's have a rest, Tom." Pip toddles over towards Dad, and Tom heads in to get a well-deserved drink.

I sit relaxing, soaking up the afternoon sun, a nice contented feeling washes over me.

"Here you are, Dad, it's orange."

"Nice one, my boy."

"Aah, that's better, thanks, Tom." My dad drains his pint of orange squash in one go.

"Right, now we are all together, I just want to have a little chat with you all, it's nothing to worry about but I need to know how you would all feel about Mum actually staying a night with us, maybe as soon as next weekend?"

My dad's words bring me crashing down to earth, my contentment vanishes. *Mum's not ready, Mum can't cope with us all, Mum can't cope.* Are my first thoughts.

"Now listen, your Mum's doing much better; she has been on this new medication for a while now, and the doctors are really pleased with her progress."

I hated myself for feeling so negative about this, but only last week at our Saturday visit, my mum hadn't really spoken, she looked distracted and frail, I couldn't see any improvement in her that day.

Tom was jumping around, even more than normal, "Mum's staying, Mum's staying."

I am happy; and confused – is that possible? The thought of Mum spending a night comes as a shock after months without Mum's familiar and constant company. Dad's proposal seems to me to be desperate and unwelcomed.

"Look, it's important that we all say something about this." I feel like Dad has already made up his mind.

Pip, who can't really say much, and Tom; well, Tom just wants his mum home, I can understand that, and want that too, but Pip and Tom don't know about Mum's suicide attempt, as far as they are concerned Tom was told that Mum has had a nervous breakdown, that she's a bit depressed and just needs a rest. That was over five months ago.

The burden of an unwanted memory, that's how it feels; I want Mum home too, but my understanding is that my mum is very ill; Dad has told me that Mum tried to kill herself again in Park Place. Dad didn't give me any details but told me this after he came home a little drunk and emotional from the Fountain Inn a few months ago.

That night, with Tom and Pip tucked up in bed, Dad had tried to explain Mum's illness. "Fran, your mum is the most beautiful person I know, she spends her time caring and showing an interest in everybody's life. Launa goes out of her way to

41

make people feel good about themselves, she loves you all, like I can't explain.

"Your mum, when aged fifteen, was an exceptional athlete, she was a sprinter, running for her county at the 100m. Not only that, she threw javelin, did the high jump and long jump; there was nothing she couldn't do. After winning medals at county level, your mum was noticed by the GB junior athletics association. They had heard about her various track and field accomplishments and invited your mum to a coaching and training weekend in London. Launa, your mum, was ecstatic; she knew she was good but couldn't believe the invitation to train and trial with the junior national team.

"Fran, your mum never made it to that invitation, she was just jogging, warming up, on your school running track, as she did religiously every night. Her leg just collapsed basically; her anterior cruciate ligament just gave way; snapped.

"Understand this, Fran, your mum, before that freak injury, was destined to represent her country in athletics, and probably become a professional athlete, her coach thought she would become a decathlete because she excelled in so many track and field events.

"Your mum has never recovered from that huge disappointment. She had surgery on her knee, but her confidence was gone, she never ran again.

Your mum took up swimming, it was a good fit, no pressure on the knee; she swam, as you know, for her county, but believe me Fran, your mum still dreamed, her only real dream was to represent her country at athletics; she always thought she would. Her dreams were crushed, she saw herself representing GB and travelling the world as a professional athlete. Mum thought she would leave our small town and get to see the world."

My dad had tears in his eyes, I started to understand more about the reason for my mum's breakdown and suicide attempt, with all that talent, and with all that in front of her, and then to have it snatched away from you in a second must be heart breaking.

"What I am trying to say, Fran, is that your mum has just reached a crossroads, she loves us all, but saw a different life for herself.

"I knew your mum was feeling low but never thought she would try to take her own life; she reached a desperate moment and just couldn't cope anymore.

"Mum and I want you to succeed, but more importantly to be happy; she wants Tom to find his way in life, outside of our small-thinking town; she wants Pip to follow her dreams and, just like me, Fran, she wants you to never to have to feel and confront such disappointments, but strive and aim for what makes you really happy."

I remember hugging Dad tightly and feeling that he must feel very alone. I told him that I love him, we both smiled, and I headed for bed, feeling sad, but a bit clearer in my head that night.

**

"Is Mum ready then, Dad? Does Mum want to spend a night?" I ask. I feel grown up, and a bit of a killjoy by asking such a difficult set of questions.

"Well as you know, Fran, I speak to Mum's doctor, Dr Linder, at least three times a week. He has suggested that a slow, night by night, homestay is the best way forward."

My Dad is speaking to me; he's not addressing Tom and Pip anymore.

I feel a pressure, a new tight chest pressing pressure, "Dad, I want Mum to come home, but is she ready, is she ready to deal with Tom, Pip, you… me?"

"I really don't know, Fran, but the doctor's think it's for the best."

I can see and sense the desperation in my dad's voice; he doesn't know if this is the best idea, how could he? But Mum's doctors have suggested a way forward, and my dad is desperate to have our mum and his wife's support.

We all sit in silence, I don't know how to feel; Tom is sipping-away on his orange juice, and Dad is rolling another fag; Pip is back in my lap, tapping her little hands onto my thighs. "Look, have a think about it, we're all seeing Mum tomorrow as you know, so let's talk about it with her and see what Mum thinks." My dad in a few sentences has tried to ease all our tensions, he's good at that. But I doubt if Mum is really going to be able to talk it through, I mean, last Saturday, Mum was feeling so ill that she didn't say more than a few words. I understand that Dad just wants the best for us all. "Look, I'm not going to say anymore, until we see how your mum is, okay?"

Dad again eases our obvious tensions, and quite selfishly I feel a sense of relief that this conversation is ending.

Dad stubs his fag out, and jumps to his feet, "Right, we all hungry? Tom, shall we take a walk down to Eddie's?"

"Sounds good, Dad, can we get a DVD from the Spar?"

"Yes, why not; you can choose a chocolate bar as well."

"Yes! Double Decker," says Tom.

"Cod, large chips and mild curry sauce for you, Fran?"

"Yes, please, Dad. Can I just have just a little bit of vinegar on mine? Eddie always puts on loads. Oh, could I get a can of coke as well, please?"

"Of course, love, not much vinegar and a coke."

Me and Pip head into the front room. Pip sits on my lap again, her chubby little legs flopping either side of mine. I scroll through the TV and only find *Come Dine With Me*; that will do.

Pip is chewing on her *SpongeBob* teddy and her little legs swing up and down. I watch a contestant cheat and spoon in shop-bought prawn cocktail into wine glasses.

***

"Eddie, how goes it mate?"

"All good, Frankie. I saw Pam and Pip dinner time. She's shooting up, got her dad's shoulders that one."

"Let's hope not, Eddie! As long as she has her mum's looks then we will be happy."

Eddie laughs and hands over a cone of chips to a customer. "Right, Frankie, usual is it?"

"You got it Eddie, three cod, three chips, one battered sausage, and three mild curry sauce. Oh, could I have less vinegar on one of the chips please."

"Less vinegar on one, no problem, mate."

"We are going to pop next door to the Spar, Eddie, okay? My Fran won her first winner's medal swimming today, so we are going to get a cake and DVD to celebrate."

"Your Fran won? Fantastic! Say congratulations from me."

"Thanks, Eddie. Will do. Right, Tom, let's head next door. If you like, you can choose the cake."

"Yeah, great; chocolate sponge cake with sprinkles please, Dad."

"Maybe, we will have a look. See you in five, Eddie."

***

My hair is dry now, but I can still smell the chlorine on my loose-fitting tracksuit; I squeeze Pip with a warming hug and kiss her head.

I can't shake Dad's words and earlier question. I have just felt the best, the best I have ever felt, after winning today, and then when Dad had proposed Mum's stay, I felt flat, unsure, full of self-doubt. To feel like that, about my own mum, I question my own thoughts and feelings Mum's return is producing in me. I flick through the channels and find nothing of any interest, so grab one of Pip's reading books off the floor and start telling her a story.

"Friday treats, Friday treats, finger fat chips, and curry sauce!" Dad and Tom stroll in, large bulging plastic bags in hand, smelling of salt and vinegar. "Chips, glorious chips, fat cod covered in Eddie's," Tom sings.

The smell is to die for. Dad begins to plate up our Friday night treat and Tom pours us all an ice-cold coke. "And for dessert, to celebrate my Fran's win, we have, picked by Tom, a chocolate slab cake with chocolate sauce, chocolate icing and chocolate sprinkles. Enjoy, my lovelies. What's on the box, Fran?"

We all settle down in front of the TV. Pip is sitting on a cushion now, with her back resting on our sofa. She's spooning in her cut up, mild curry-sauce-covered, battered sausage, and I notice her little toes moving; contented, I think to myself. Me, Dad and Tom have a tray each; we normally eat around the kitchen table during the week, Dad insists on that, but Friday is different, Friday is treat night. Our plates are full, Eddie doesn't believe in small portions.

Dad says, "Let's put the film on shall we, after our supper?"

"Sounds good, Dad. What did you get?"

"A classic, my love; the one and only *Dodgeball*. I know we've all seen it, but that was ages ago, remember, when Mum was at home."

I laugh out loud, just the thought of seeing Ben Stiller again in his tight silver lycra makes me chuckle. We all start to tuck into our Friday night treat, loving every mouthful of our huge, tasty fish supper.

I take the empty plates out to the kitchen, and when putting them into the sink I can't help but notice my bulging belly, Eddie's fish suppers are to die for, and Fridays are the best.

Dad comes into the kitchen and starts to cut up the chocolate cake, he adds huge amounts of squirty cream to each bowl. "Let's raise our bowls to Fran, a super swimming star; your mum's going to be so proud of you, love."

I feel special, and love the feeling of winning, but deep in the back of my head all I can really think about is Mum. We all take our seats and Dad pushes play on the remote as we all get comfortable, bellies full to bursting from our Friday Night's treats.

Chapter 3

"Mum, Mum, I can't see you, where are you?"

"Tom, Tom, wake up its just a dream." I hold firmly on to Tom's arms as he thrusts his body from side to side, his forehead is covered in sweat, his pyjamas feel damp to the touch. I notice Tom's bedside light; it's still alight but lying on his bedroom floor.

"It's okay, Tom, it's just a dream." I try to wipe the sweat off Tom's forehead with one of his worn, crumpled-up T-shirts.

"Fran, I could see Mum. She's so far away, she's wearing all white, I can see bright flowers, I can smell bleach or… or disinfectant."

I loosen my grip on Tom's skinny arms. "It's okay, Tom. It's Saturday; we get to see Mum today." Tom is sitting up now, resting his head firmly on his slatted wooden headboard.

"I can't see Mum anymore, Fran."

I pick up Tom's light and place it back on his bedside table. "Budge over, Tom." I sit myself on Tom's bed and rest my head against his wooden bed frame. It can only be the early hours of Saturday morning, I guess, as I notice the pitch-black night out of Tom's bedroom window; there is an orange glow from our streetlights reflecting their false warmth through his window and onto his bedroom wall. I hold onto Tom's hand; it feels clammy and hot; we both just lie there comforting each other without talking.

I was awoken earlier by a sound. At first it sounded like Pip crying, but as I came out of my sleep, the sound sounded different; the cry was deeper, louder, like a moan, a man's moan.

Wide awake now, I first thought it might be Dad, then as I stood up out of my bed the noise seemed to be coming from Tom's room, which is directly opposite mine.

I zipped up my hoodie, feeling the cold of the night, wiped the sleep out of my eyes and headed quietly towards Tom's room.

This is the first time I have ever had to see to Tom. There was a time when Mum was first committed to Park Place that I had to comfort Pip. She would scream; I mean scream her lungs out; how Dad and Tom slept through that I'll never know.

"It's okay, Tom, it's just a dream."

"Is Mum coming home, Fran?" Tom breaks the night's silence with a question I can't truly answer.

"I don't know, Tom, let's see how today goes. You feeling okay? You had a nightmare?"

"Just tired, Fran, but I don't want to sleep, I don't want those dreams again. What time is it?"

"It's only early, Tom, we must try to get some more sleep."

"I know, can you stay with me?"

I don't want to, but of course I do; Tom rarely asks for my help or advice on anything, so this hits me hard, I suddenly feel emotional, tears well up in my tired eyes.

I turn Tom's bedside light off, and he turns over to the left, I stay upright, I can't see myself sleeping tonight. I try to relax but can't focus on anything but seeing Mum later today, the idea of her coming home makes me feel uncomfortable for some reason, the thought of it makes my stomach begin to ache, and I have a peculiar tingle in my legs. I spend the rest of the night tossing and turning, unable to switch off. Tom is sound asleep as I notice the first light break through his window.

Bacon smells good, doesn't it? Cooking bacon and brewing coffee smell great. Nearly every Saturday morning Dad cooks us all a fry-up.

"Wake up, Tom; wake up, Fran."

I don't think that Dad has even noticed that I'm not in my bedroom. I can hear the TV downstairs; Pip must be up; I hear the high-pitched tones of *Teletubbies*; *Teletubbies'* Po!

I stretch my arms and then turn my head from side to side; Tom is still asleep, he's lying in the same position as last night, apart from his toes are now poking out from the bottom of the duvet.

"Fran, Fran, coffee is ready."

Dad makes a large, strong pot of coffee on a Saturday morning. Normally it's down to me to make a cuppa during the week, and I usually just make tea. Me and Tom have black tea while I make Pip a milky, lukewarm cup. So, having a proper cup of coffee is a real treat, I love my coffee and the intoxicating smell makes me get up this morning.

I nudge Tom in his back, and he starts to stir. He slowly stretches his legs out and gives out a big yawn. I slowly get up myself and head towards the bathroom. I take a look at my reflection in the bathroom mirror and don't like what's looking back. In that moment I picture the day ahead, this day is going to be hard, I'm not looking forward to it.

"You okay, love? Did you sleep well?"

"Yeah, I slept okay, thanks Dad. Pip, Pip the orange Pip what you watching? *Teletubbies*, 'tubbies again!" I grab, tickle and kiss Pip all in one go. She giggles, rolls over and we both lay flat on our backs on the front room floor. I tickle Pip's tummy again and she gives out the cutest sounding laugh.

"You ready for breakfast, you lot?"

Tom comes bounding down the stairs, still in his pyjamas and he gives out a big brekkie cry,

"Sausages, Dad, sausages for me!" He misses the bottom three steps and crashes into the door, "Sausages, sausages."

I pick up Pip and carry her towards our kitchen; Dad has laid out the table, we have table mats, knives and forks, of course, red and brown sauce, and even serviettes.

I drain my first cup of coffee and butter my toast; Dad's brekkies are great, always too much though, he always cooks so much. I remember when Mum would cook our fry-ups, she would grill everything, I think Dad enjoys his Saturday mornings, he loves cooking a fry-up for all of us.

I cut up Pip's sausages and bacon and make soldiers of her toast; Dad is full of energy this morning; he slurps his coffee from his man-sized coffee mug. "Ahh! Pass the butter please, Fran."

I notice Tom stuffing oversized pieces of sausage into the side of his mouth while using his knife to slice up his bacon and eggs. Pip starts to swing her little legs, *she looks so content,* I think, whilst she's chewing on her buttered toast.

I am less content, my thoughts are fuzzy; my stomach starts to rumble as I push my eggs around my plate, no appetite suddenly, I feel a little sick, I am not looking forward to the day ahead.

I think Dad must have used every pot and pan in the house. Beans are stuck hard to our little wooden-handled saucepan, the frying pan holds the charred remains of fried bacon, sausages and eggs. I finish the washing up and try to convince Tom it is time to get ready.

Pip is my next mission this morning. "Come on, orange Pip, let's get you ready." Dad is outside dragging on a fag, he's on his mobile phone; the way the conversation is going I guess he is talking to Aunty Pam.

I start to give Pip a flannel wash, she giggles when I wash under her chin. "Tickles, tickles," I laugh out loud, "I've got to wash you, love; lift your head." I gently pinch her nose and ruffle her thick blond hair.

"Pip is almost sorted, Dad; she's coming down the stairs. Can you watch her while I get ready?"

"Thanks, Fran, just spoke to Aunty Pam, she's going to pop round later."

Great, excellent, I sarcastically think to myself.

I jump out of the shower and begin drying my body, "Tom, Tom, you getting ready?" No reply, so I begin to dry my hair. "Tom, you ready?"

The silence just hangs in the air; I wrap myself up in a towel. "Tom, can I come in?" There's no answer so I tap my knuckles on Tom's door and start to push it open.

I don't see him at first, for one moment I think he must be outside, maybe kicking a football around, then I see an uneven shape hidden, wrapped up under the duvet.

"I don't want to go, I can't go. Tell Mum I am sick, I've got a stomach bug." Tom raises his head from under the duvet, then rubs his stomach as to convince himself of his own sickness.

"Tom, I can't cope with this today. Mum's expecting us all; Dad's almost ready to go, Pip is dressed, I am nearly ready; I understand today is going to be hard, but let's just see how Mum is. Let's just please see how things are."

I am so frustrated, I have a picture of our day ahead, and Tom's refusal to go is not part of that picture. Tom has never refused to see Mum before, this only heightens my own peculiar feelings, my body feels tingly, but not in a nice way. It feels similar to the time I drank too much caffeine at Tanya's; I didn't realize then about the caffeine buzz. We helped ourselves to Tanya's Dad's Red Bulls; we had three cans each and loads of chocolate whilst watching a re-run of *Twilight*. I felt so sick, sick to the stomach and got no sleep that night.

Dad's words to us all last night have really brought up some unwanted feelings, for us all, I think. Tom is confused, I am confused, Pip is, well Pip, but I feel angry, and I keep feeling strange this morning, like my heart is missing a beat or something. *Maybe it's because I didn't get much sleep last night.*

"Tom, we have got to go; Mum's expecting to see us all today, and Dad's so excited, he thinks Mum is ready, ready to stay a night. I don't know if that's true, but please let's just go, let's see."

Tom takes some persuading, but he finally begins to get dressed. I leave Tom to grunt and groan whilst getting himself ready.

"Come on you two, it's nearly nine o'clock." Dad is so eager to get going, we normally leave around eight forty-five. Dad's never late for anything, but this morning with Tom not wanting to go, and me having to wash-up every saucepan in the house we are definitely running a little late.

Park Place, Mum's hospital, is only about ten miles away; the old grey granite building stands within a large wood on the edge of Dartmoor. Visiting times over the weekend are ten o'clock to four o'clock. Dad, though, always gets us there too early. I don't get that, it just seems to add to the tension, the anticipation; Pip and Tom get bored, and I normally spend my time feeling a bit edgy, even a little nervous.

I hear Tom shut his bedroom door and then bound down the stairs. I feel rushed, I hate that.

"Come on, Fran, we're ready apart from you."

"Okay! Okay, nearly ready, Dad." I pull on my jeans quickly, struggling to do up the metal buttons. My make-up's already done, so I quickly make a ponytail of my still damp hair, grab my phone, slipping it naturally into my jeans back pocket. "Coming."

When I get to the bottom of the stairs, Dad is already pulling on Pip's pink coat, "Put your arms out, love. Come on, Fran, we're just waiting on you."

I can tell Dad's keen to get going, but sometimes I don't think he understands what I go through. This morning I haven't had the time to mention Tom's nightmare, or his refusal at first to go. I am feeling rushed; I hate being rushed!

"I am ready!" I say it with no warmth at all; in fact, I shock myself with how bitter and cold my words just sounded. Tom gives me a sideways glance; I think he noticed. Dad pulls the kitchen window shut and then turns the TV off. "Right, let's just go."

"Dad, can I sit in the front? Fran did last Saturday."

To be honest I don't care this morning, I would rather sit in the back with Pip and daydream out the window.

"Yes, Tom, it's your turn."

Dad and Tom start to get into the front seats. Our car is a relic, an old beat up Volvo Estate, dark blue in colour, it has flaking rust all around the black plastic door handles and smells damp inside. I open the boot and put Pip's pushchair in, the door as usual gives out a high-pitched squeak.

Pip strapped in and seat belts on, we are ready to go.

Our once-a-week journey to Park Place takes us through narrow, high-hedged roads; the road winds its way through two small villages, past them we then take a left onto a main road; that road takes us over a cattle grid, which marks the start of Dartmoor.

The journey this morning is unusually quiet, I spend most of my time looking and daydreaming out of the window; Tom is playing on his phone; Pip is happily chewing on a biscuit, and Dad is blowing smoke out of his window.

"Dad, can we stop? I need a wee."

"Can't you hold on, Tom? We are nearly there."

"I can't, I need to go, I really need to go."

Dad swerves abruptly, recklessly towards a farmer's gate. "Go, if you got to go!"

"Dad, what are you doing! We're not going to be late; we can't see Mum until ten anyway."

"I don't want to be late, Fran. Mum's expecting us."

The atmosphere, the anticipation this morning is different; everything feels different.

After last night, when Dad spoke to us all, my first reaction was fear, the fear of change. Mum's illness and committal have taken our rock away.

Mum was for all of us the voice, the compassionate and caring voice.

Mum's been away from us for over five months now. Since then we all have changed; me and Tom don't really speak, not like we used to anyway; Pip is less affected I think, but I don't know. Dad just buries himself into his work, sometimes working sixty, seventy hours a week.

We all have, over time, got used to Mum's absence, but the routines which we have grown into lack the fun and comfort of the past. It's tough, it's the uncertainty of what is to come that scares me the most; Dad really needs Mum home, I think; we all do.

Tom zips up and then quickly, awkwardly does up his seat belt.

"Right can we go now? Does anyone else want to make us late?"

Shaking my head, I turn my attentions toward Pip, she's so quiet, just sitting there pulling and then bouncing her *Square Bob* teddy against the car window.

Dad still puffing on his roll-up takes a right and I notice the old wooden Park Place sign in the distance; my stomach turns over and I find myself swallowing hard. The tingle in my legs return.

We turn left onto the straight tree-lined drive that leads us up towards the car park. Dad parks like he always does at the far end of the car park, as far away from the hospital entrance as possible! Tom stops playing on his game; looks at his phone, "Nine forty-five, Dad. Can we go to the gardens?"

"Not yet, Tom, let's just wait. We can see the gardens later."

The silence is deafening; the clock on our car's dashboard seems to be going backwards. I am not sure why we have to just sit here, sitting silently in the car. I instinctively pull my mobile out, I have some Facebook updates; Tanya has posted a picture of herself, she is in her pyjamas, but her face is fully made-up. I post a comment, *Ready for what? gorgeous though cu l8tr.*

I undo Pip's car seat. She raises up her arms. "You are free, little Pip, free."

Dad does up his window as Tom opens his door. "Right, let's go see Donnie; let him know we are here."

Donnie is Park Place's security guard. He is a huge round man; he always seems to have a sweaty forehead, and his uniform looks creased. He sits in the foyer next to the reception. I often think if anyone wanted to do a runner, Donnie would be the most ill-equipped person to catch someone.

Dad pushes the buzzer on the wall. "Morning, Donnie, it's Frankie. We are a bit early."

"No problems, come on in."

The first thing you notice when opening the heavy wooden door is the smell; it's cabbage, disinfectant and old books. There is a waiting area, with a mismatch of chairs and old magazines on a glass table.

"Morning, Frankie, Fran, nice to see you. Just have a seat, won't be long."

More waiting, more silence.

I flip through a December issue of *Bella* magazine, Pip is on Dad's lap, and Tom returns to his game.

"Nice weather, not too humid this morning."

"Yeah, nice breeze this morning, Donnie."

The buzzer hums, and Donnie returns to his desk. "Morning, come on in."

We are joined by two elderly women. They are both carrying Bags for Life; I can see packs of biscuits and bubble bath poking out the top of one of the bags.

"Oh, she's lovely; what's her name?"

"Pip, Pippa. She's got her mum's good looks, thank God."

"Oh, bless; lovely name."

Donnie reappears with his clipboard. "Right, folks, sign your life away."

Every Saturday he says that. I always think Donnie's choice of words are a bit weird, but Dad grabs the biro, which is attached to the clipboard by a piece of string and signs us in. The elderly ladies take an age to decide who should sign Donnie's clipboard; in the end they both decide to.

Donnie pushes open the glass double doors which lead us into the main corridor, from there it's just a few steps before we reach the dayroom.

At first I don't see Mum, then I hear her. "Aah, Pip. Come give Mum a cuddle."

Mum is still in her dressing gown, not a great sign.

Pip reacts and waddles her way toward Mum. Mum lifts up Pip and raises her high into the air. Tom follows closely behind and hugs them both as Pip is safely in Mum's arms.

Me and Dad head over; Mum gives Dad a kiss on his cheek and grabs my arm. "Good to see you all." Mum looks thin, her face is drawn, and her touch is cold.

"We got here early, Mum. So excited to see you."

"I know, Tom; I've been excited too. I got up at seven this morning."

We all sit down. The dayroom is huge, high ceilings with dusty chandeliers. Mum, Pip and Dad sit back on the dark brown, scratched leather sofa; Me and Tom rest into the soft armchairs opposite.

My attention is drawn to the far side of the room, it's Edna; Edna has been here for over five years, Mum had told us. The first time I became aware of Edna was at our first visit to see Mum. I remember the heavy wooden doors, the waiting, then the dayroom, it was so full. At first I thought seeing Mum would be in a quiet room, a comfortable family room, just us and maybe a doctor. So, when we couldn't find Mum amongst the busy dayroom visitors and patients, I first became aware of Edna. At that time a noise grabbed my attention, Edna was surrounded by four or five white uniforms, the noise was a high-pitched moan, a cat-like cry.

"Let's go, Ed; let's get you to your room."

"No... no... it's not my room. Don't put me there, don't look at me, don't put me back there," I remember her saying.

Edna looked old. I mean she looked older than her skin looked; her hair was dank and greasy, her eyes looked wide; black, huge, vacant eyes.

In the end Edna was removed, the staff just lifted her up like a piece of furniture, her legs never touched the ground, the doors seemed to open automatically, Edna was gone.

"How have you been, Fran?"

"Good, Mum. Swimming's going well; I won yesterday."

"Wow, great news, that's brilliant, Fran."

"We celebrated with a cake, Mum, a big chocolate cake, didn't we, Fran?"

"Yeah, first Eddie's fish supper, followed by a huge slice of cake and cream. I still feel so full up!"

"We had a nice night, Launa, a special Friday night, treat night, so proud of Fran."

"I wish I could have been there love; next time, next time."

I feel agitated, I don't know how to feel about all this attention, I feel myself start to blush.

"There will be other times, love. Fran's training so hard; next stop the Olympics!"

"Oh, Dad, stop please."

"Tom, what have you been up to, love?"

"Well… playing football with Noah mainly, also playing on my Xbox; Noah's lending me his new *Call of Duty* game later."

"That's an eighteen game, isn't? All guns and violence."

"It is. All the kids are playing it though, love; I only let Tom play it a few hours a week."

"Well as long as you think it's okay, Frankie."

An awkward moment is interrupted by the familiar sound of the tea trolley. The wheels on the old wooden trolley squeak and rattle so loudly, heard even above the filling day room and its many noises and ongoing conversations. I hear Gladys and her distinctive high pitch voice offering coffee and cake to the table opposite us. "We have carrot cake today, it's homemade; sugar and milk in your drinks, my loves?"

"Do you want anything, kids? Launa, what about you?"

"Just a tea."

"Can I have cake, Dad?"

"Nothing for me, Dad; maybe just get Pip a Fruit Shoot."

Dad gives Gladys our order and she cuts an extra-large slice of cake for Tom, giving him a wink as she passes over the plate. "Enjoy."

After his coffee Dad suggests that I take Tom and Pip over to the kiddie's corner. The kiddie's corner is full of old donated toys and books, also there are two brightly coloured bean bags and a broken doll's house.

I take Pip's hand and lead her towards the corner. Tom runs in front heading straight for the empty bean bags. As we approach, I notice two toddlers playing with some building blocks. They are dressed in the same way; the smaller of the two, a girl, keeps knocking down the tower. She lets out a loud giggle as her brother waves his arm as to discourage the demolition.

Me and Pip take a seat on the carpeted floor. I grab the nearest book and start reading the story; Tom is happily lounging on the bean bags and playing on his phone.

***

"Kids are looking well; Pip's getting so tall."

"They are doing all right, love. How are things with you? I have missed you."

"Oh, love, I've missed you all, as always. Last Saturday I was feeling down, detached, I hope the kids didn't notice."

"They didn't say anything. I think Fran mentioned you seemed a bit quiet, but that was all."

"This new medication is making me feel so tired. It's helping a bit, but I do feel tired, I'm sleeping a lot."

"Doctor Linder said that this new medication might do that, didn't he?"

"He did, but I also feel numb, I can't see clearly. My week's been hard, love; I think the thought of coming home for a night is playing on my mind."

"Do you want to?"

"I do, I do. I just don't know if I am ready though."

"Oh, love; I had a chat with the kids last night, I told them that maybe you're ready to stay a night."

"Why did you do that? I didn't promise, did I? Doctor Linder thinks it's a good idea, but I've got to feel ready; I've got to make that decision."

"We've talked about it, love. We've talked it through with Doctor Linder. This is what we all have been working towards. I need you home, love."

"Frankie, the pressure you put on me… Well, I just can't cope with it."

***

"Well, Pip, let's choose another story." Pip waddles off to find another book. I glance over towards Mum and Dad. Dad seems strained; his forehead is resting in his hands and he is sitting forward, looking downwards to the carpeted floor.

"Found one, Fran."

"Great." Pip passes me a tatty looking *Beano* annual. As I grab for it, I notice the toddlers have moved on from small demolition to full on fisticuffs. Tom giggles at the miniature boxing bout taking place. I stand up, intending to break up the fight.

"Lily! Max! Stop it." A slim, tall woman quickly arrives. The day room is filling up fast and the woman has to excuse herself whilst squeezing past the seated people. "Stop it, you two." She grabs them both, pulling the toddlers apart. "I am so embarrassed; they always do this. Sorry, all." The toddlers start to cry at the same time, a double dose of loud shrieking and wailing.

"It's okay; they both most get a bit bored?"

"They do, but we are only here for an hour or so. Come on, you two. Leave these nice people in peace."

As I settle down with Pip again, I see Dad hugging Mum. I can't really tell but I think Mum is crying.

"I don't want to put any more pressure on you, love, I just miss you being around. I can't begin to understand how you must be really feeling. I try my hardest with the kids, and your sister is an amazing help. Pam gives so much time and support, but I miss my wife. I know that's pressure, but it's the truth; we've always spoken the truth to one another."

"We do, I do. I can't stop feeling anxious though. I wake up, and for a split second I seem normal. Then I notice my legs, they seem heavy with an uncomfortable ache, my arms start to have pins and needles, then my thoughts take over, my heart begins to race, my stomach turns. I can't explain how my body feels, let alone what's going on in my mind."

"Launa, what can I do? I just want to make you better, I feel helpless."

"I know you and the kids are here for me, love, but not being able... capable, to be a normal kind of Mum is killing me inside."

"The counselling seemed to be helping you though. What about the cognitive therapy? That was working, wasn't it?"

"I am still having my one-to-ones with Doctor Linder, but this past week I haven't been well enough to join the group sessions. I can't face that. I don't think I can do that anymore, Frankie."

"Okay', let's have a break, shall we? Head out for a walk, it's such a lovely day. We can talk more in a bit."

***

"Fran, you okay? Shall we have some fresh air, have a walk in the garden?"

"You both all right?" I ask. "Yeah, I think Pip and Tom could do with going outside."

"We are just talking some things through, love. Yes, some fresh air is a good idea, I was just suggesting that to your mother. Get Pip and Tom and meet us out the back."

I can see Dad is upset. He doesn't make eye contact with me and looks uncomfortable. Mum's eyes are red, and her face looks puffy.

"I'll see you all in the garden, just popping to the loo."

Dad heads off, and Mum walks with me towards the kiddie's corner. "Is Dad okay?"

"He's fine, love. It's hard you know, it's hard for all of us."

"Come on, little Pip, Tom; let's see the gardens."

The tall, glass double doors open outwards to a large paved patio area, the steps heading onto the lawn are steep and half-moon in shape. Tom jumps two at a time and rolls headfirst onto freshly cut grass.

"Tom, be careful."

The gardens at Park Place are beautiful, especially in the summer; lots of colour, lots of green trees. Rose beds separate the lawn; beyond them is a large pond, with huge lily pads floating on the top.

"Let's go see the fish, Mum. Can you remember when Pip tried to feed the fish grass?"

"Oh yes, bless her; I think the fish got a bit confused that day."

"Come catch me, Pip." Tom sprints off. Pip can't find her feet quickly enough as she giggles, falls over and excitedly moves forward.

"Go on, Pip. Get him."

I feel the morning sun on my face; it feels nice and warm. The cut grass smell enters my nostrils, and I can hear various birds as they fly above.

"How's Dad been, Fran?"

"Okay, I think. He gets so excited about seeing you, Mum. He got all emotional yesterday, after my win. You know Dad, he doesn't really show his emotions that often."

"Your dad's a sensitive soul at heart, love. He keeps things locked up, but he feels everything."

"He's been working some long hours. I think he's in work tomorrow. Is Pam coming to see you tomorrow?"

"Yeah, we are going to have a walk together, down to Frew's Slope. She's planning a picnic, I think. I can't eat much though, Fran. This new medication is upsetting my belly."

"Dad said it was helping, he said Doctor Linder thought you should come home; maybe stay a night."

"I know, love, I've just been talking to Dad about that. To be honest I am not sure. Dad's upset, but I don't know if I am ready yet."

Strangely, Mum's words ease some of my concerns. I am confused though, I thought Mum was definitely up for a staying a night with us.

I see Tom out of the corner of my eye, but my attention is drawn towards the flowers, they begin to look distorted. I feel a dull pain in my arms and my chest suddenly feels tight, I begin to notice that I am feeling unusually hot. I begin sweating, the flowers seem to be a mass, just a mass of blurred colour.

I shake my head, and then rub my eyes, an overwhelming feeling comes over me, a rush of fear makes me take a deep breath.

"You all right, Fran?"

"I need to sit down, Mum." *I need to be on my own,* is my real first thought. "Yeah, I'll be ok, just need to go to the toilet I think."

I head off quickly, making my way towards the toilets, not needing to pee, just needing to be on my own all of a sudden. I walk fast towards the toilets, which are in the main corridor. I don't make eye contact with anyone as I quickly make my way through the dayroom. I shut the cubicle door and sit down on the closed toilet seat. My head is full of a million thoughts, none of which I can focus on. I notice my breathing, it's fast and loud like when I push hard with my swimming strokes.

My message tone sounds; it makes me jump; the sound seems so loud; I can't even look at the message. I hear the main toilet door open; it makes me hold my breath, I notice every sound, I become aware of a sickly bleach and urine smell. It takes an age for the person to flush the loo and then wash their hands. As the door slams shut, I release a big chest-filled breath. What's going on? I want to go home; I need to go home.

***

"Where's Fran?"

"She's just popped to the loo. Shall we have a seat, a fag and wait for her here then?"

"Sounds good."

"Tom. Pip, me and Dad are having a seat, don't go out of sight please."

"Okay, Mum."

***

I wonder if the sausages or bacon were off, have I got food poisoning, I have never had that before, is this what that feels like? That must be it. I take a pee and begin to feel a bit clearer in my thoughts. My chest still feels tight as I flush the loo. As I wash my hands and wet my face my blurred vision goes away; *I've got food poisoning, I will be okay.*

The thought of walking through the busy day room again, and out towards the gardens doesn't appeal so I take the long way around, passing Donnie and the reception area. "You okay there?"

"Yes, just going to the car, then heading to the gardens to catch up with them all."

"Great; lovely day for being outside."

I walk the length of the building, passing the reserved parking for staff. I then walk under the arched side entrance to the gardens. I see Mum and Dad in the distance, I hear Tom, and my thoughts turn to how I explain how I am feeling, I don't want to cut our visit short, but my food poisoning is not going away. I swallow hard and rub my belly.

"Here she is, we thought we had lost you down the lavvy, love!"

"You okay? You look a bit pale, Fran."

"Not feeling great, Mum, feel a little sick to be honest, I wonder if it's something I've ate."

"We've all eaten the same love; I feel fine, Tom and Pip seem okay. Look, they are running around like racehorses."

My Dad's words don't help, I doubt my symptoms now. Maybe it was the food at school, no one else here has had that.

"Have a seat, love, you will be okay, just take a minute." *It's going to take more than a minute*; I think to myself. "Me and your mum are going to grab Pip's pushchair and then take them both for a walk into the forest; you coming?"

"I think I may just stay here for a little while; can I catch you up in a bit?"

"Yes, love, of course, we will take the bottom path, you know the one, it starts behind the car park; that small path that takes you along the riverbank."

"Okay, see you in a bit."

"Is Fran all right, Mum?"

"Yes, Tom, I think she's just a little tired, love; maybe all that food you ate last night has upset her stomach as well."

"We did eat a lot, I had two huge helpings of cake with squirty cream."

"Well, Fran will be okay, she's going to catch us up. Let's pop to the car, you can help me with the pushchair."

***

I feel strange, I take some time just tensing my leg muscles; they feel tight and heavy, my heart is racing like a fast, repetitive drumbeat. My message tone sounds again, I guess it's just Tanya and will answer when I feel more together. Still sitting, I feel drawn into feeling my chest, my skin is so damp and feels hot to the touch, I can feel my heart pounding faster now, it beats loudly in my ears. I want to go home. The thought of slipping under my duvet is all I can think about. I stand up abruptly, hoping somehow to shake off this peculiar feeling; suddenly I am off balance, my head is spinning so I widen my stance as to re-balance myself, my arms seem heavy and I sense a tingle all over my body, I feel a single drop of sweat run down my back.

***

"Tom, did you see the kingfisher? It just flew down the river."

"I missed it, Mum, will we see it again?"

"Oh, maybe; they are quite rare though. Did you see it, Frankie?"

"I did, I caught a glimpse then it was gone. I wish Fran was here, she would have loved that."

"I know, she loves seeing the wildlife, that's only the second time I've ever seen one here."

"This is lovely, Launa, I really miss our walks. I take the kids on the moor when I can; they love Haytor and the surrounding moorland, the views from up there are amazing. Tom and Fran always climb the tor while me and Pip just sit and watch."

"The moors are fantastic, I miss our long walks too, especially the visit to the pub to refresh ourselves after."

"Yeah, plenty of refreshment taken I remember, do you remember that strong ale you tried? Wacker, it was called I think."

"I do. God, I slept all the way home, six percent wasn't it?"

"It was six percent and thick as treacle."

***

I wonder if Dad has left the car open, he normally locks it when outside ours, but he may have forgotten to do it here. I make my mind up to go and have a look, if I could just sit in the safety and comfort of the car for a while, that would help; surely that would help.

I raise myself up from the bench, I could take the same route I took earlier, save going through the busy day room and seeing anybody.

***

"Throw your stick in, Pip; you too, Tom. Let's see which one makes the footbridge first."

"Mine will, my stick is going to win."

"We'll see; on my count, get ready 3,2,1 go!"

"Good throw, Pip, look yours is winning."

"Winning, mine winning."

***

I retrace my earlier steps and make my way towards the car park; I hear the muffled sounds of the dayroom and notice a few people have come outside and are sitting on the mis-matched patio chairs.

The sun is hot on my face and I squint as I take a left towards the archway, "Oh, sorry, sorry Dr Linder." I almost knock Dr Linder over as I pass through the narrow opening.

"It's okay, Fran, how are you?" I didn't expect to see anybody, let alone speak, so Dr Linder's question throws me into an immediate panic.

"Yeah, doing okay thanks; just heading to the car to get something."

"Nice to see you, Fran. I am going to catch up with you all later, did Mum say?"

"Um, I don't think so."

"Okay, nothing to worry about, just wanted to see you all together. See you later, bye."

Yes, the car is unlocked, I feel at first a huge sense of relief, I take a seat in the back and then almost immediately feel stupid. What am I doing? Am I hiding? Am I going crazy? Suddenly I feel really self-conscious, what if people see me just sitting here alone, what would they think? The sanctuary of the car has now become a goldfish bowl, my heart pounds loud again, and I notice my top as it rises and falls with my uncontrollable heartbeat. I can't see straight, my vision is blurred, so I rub my eyes as if to clear my eyesight. I decide to give my dad a call, he needs to know that I'm not feeling so good and will be wondering where I've got to.

Dad, come on Dad, answer your phone. My signal is so weak, so I get out of the car, and in hope more than anything I hold out my phone until I have a few bars, finally I get a signal...

"Love, you okay? Where are you?"

"Dad, I don't feel very well, I think I really do have food poisoning or something."

"Oh, Fran, where are you?"

"By the car, I am so sorry."

"Don't be silly, I am on my way."

***

"Launa, that was Fran, she's not feeling too good. I'm going to see what's going on; you staying here for a bit?"

"Yeah, will do."

"Tom, look after your little sister; just popping to get Fran."

"Okay, Dad."

***

After my brief chat with Dad I start to feel a little calmer, I take a couple of deep breaths, my heart rate has definitely slowed down, and my vision seems a little clearer. Resting against the car I take a look at my phone, two messages both from Tanya, *"Hi u you out l8tr xx,"* *"Fran msg me, going xx out…drinks etc! xx."* Tanya's messages are always short, straight to the point, that always surprises me. Tanya can talk, I mean talk a lot, once she starts, she just doesn't stop.

"Tan not feeling great, txt u when home," I press send and notice Dad coming.

"Fran, you okay, love? What's up?"

Uncontrollably, I start crying, really crying from somewhere deep inside. I wrap my arms tightly around Dad; I smell tobacco mixed with apple shower gel on his clothing.

"Oh, love, what is it?"

"I don't know, Dad. I feel weird, dizzy, my heart keeps pounding."

"Okay, okay, just breathe, deep breaths, love. You are going to be fine."

Dad's words help; I start taking deep breaths as I pull away from Dad's chest,

"You've been so busy, Fran, you know; swimming, looking after Tom and Pip, the house; I think you have just worn yourself out. And seeing Mum, seeing her in here is hard."

"Maybe, but I've never felt this way before, it could be food poisoning, couldn't it?"

My dad shrugs his large shoulders and gives out a quiet sigh. "Maybe; it could be, do you feel sick? Is your stomach playing up?"

"A little. I've been sweating a lot and my arms and legs feel really heavy."

"Okay, I think let's just rest here a moment, keep doing your breathing; just focus on that, love."

Dad's calming presence and my focused breathing are helping; my normal senses seem to be returning, I feel awake again now, like I've just come out of a deep restful sleep; my eyes feel clearer, and my body feels like mine again, not all heavy, awkward and off balanced, my sweating has stopped too.

"You got some colour back in your cheeks, Fran. Hey, I think you snotted on my new shirt with that cuddle; look it's like a slug trail." I laugh, Dad pulls a disgusted looking face and we both laugh; laugh out loud.

"Let's have a wander, breathe in the fresh air, let the sun dry my snot-covered shirt."

"Yeah, okay." Dad takes my arm; he doesn't do that too often, it makes me feel happy, I feel warm, I feel safe, I'm going to be okay.

***

"Throw your sticks in again. This time, Tom, do it together at the same time as your sister, please"

"I did, Pip was just slow."

"Well, just make sure you don't throw before I say three. Look, here's your dad and Fran coming now; wait for them to get here then I'll do the countdown."

"We're back."

"You okay, Fran? I was getting worried."

"Much better, Mum. Not sure what it was but I feel a lot better."

"Probably all that food from last night."

"Yeah, I guess. I bumped into Dr Linder; he said hello and mentioned that he was seeing us all later."

"Yeah, didn't I mention that?"

"Don't think so, I can't remember."

"Well, he just wants to have a talk; talk about me staying a night, maybe next weekend."

"Mum, Mum, we are ready!"

"Okay, 3,2,1 go!"

I knew, of course, the subject of Mum coming home was going to be talked about; I really don't know how to feel about that. Mum seems okay today, but I know that can all change in a blink of an eye. My stomach turns over again, I concentrate my attention towards Tom and Pip playing, but suddenly feel a strange twinge in my arms and legs, my heart seems to skip a beat.

I watch Tom and Pip continue to play sticks, whilst Dad makes Mum and him a roll-up. "After our fag, shall we head back, get a drink or something?"

"Can do. What time are we seeing Dr Linder?"

"Twelve o'clock. His office is pretty small, so he said to meet in the therapy room."

We all slowly make our way back towards Park Place. I walk arm in arm with my mum, which feels nice; Dad is pushing Pip and Tom is way in front hitting tall weeds with a stick he found next to the riverbank.

"So proud of you, Fran. I bet it felt great to win; was Tanya second?"

"She was, it was close, but I finished strongly, she wasn't happy, but I don't care about that, I've trained so hard, I knew I could win, Mum."

"You are strong-willed, love; I've always known that you have had to deal with so much, I find it hard to cope with you know, how much you must do at home without your mother being around."

I can see Mum welling up; she rubs her forehead and bites her bottom lip, "It's okay, Mum; really it's okay. I don't do everything; Dad is always there; Pam helps as well."

"I know, love, but it should be me. I should be there taking care of you all. I want to do that; I want to come home to do that."

"We all want you home, Mum, back home and well. Let's see what Dr Linder thinks, maybe coming home one day at a time is best; just see how you feel."

"You're getting so grown up, love. You're right, let's talk to Dr Linder about it all."

It's nearing midday so after our cold drinks from the vending machine we head through the wide corridors, past the small offices and into the therapy room; we are a little early, so the room is empty. In the therapy room there are about a dozen chairs, a couple of tables and some weird-looking art on the walls. The carpet looks worn, and it has that disinfectant smell which seems to linger everywhere in this place.

***

"Hello, hello everyone, forgive me I am running a little late, it's so nice to see you all together." Dr Linder has a strong, different sounding accent, Swedish I think. He's always in a suit, a crumpled brown or grey suit, he has a thick unkempt greying beard and his ears are full of white wispy hair. He wears thin-framed rectangular glasses which are always resting on the end of his nose. I like Dr Linder, there's a friendliness about him, a humorous character I imagine, he has a cheeky welcoming grin on his face nearly every time I've seen him.

"I don't want to keep you too long, it's a lovely sunny day, a great day for being outside. It's important I think to have a chat all together. Firstly, it would be helpful to hear how things are with you, Frankie? Just feel free to talk openly."

"Ah, that's tough, Doctor, I don't know where to start."

"Okay, well maybe just talk about this week, how have things been?"

"Well, it's been a busy week as usual, the kids have had school, Fran's been busy training after school for her swim meet, which she won."

"Fantastic, Fran; that must have felt good?"

"It did, it felt really good."

"I bet you do some miles in that pool?"

"Quite a few, a couple miles a day, I think."

"Impressive stuff, Fran. Launa, you must be proud of Fran?"

"Very, very proud of Fran's commitment. I know how much it takes out of you, all that training, diet and focus."

"We celebrated with a cake, didn't we, Dad?"

"We did, Tom; you and Pip had a face full of chocolate cake, didn't you?"

"Yes, and cream."

"Well, that sounds tasty. Now, like I said, I don't want to keep you here for too long. From my point of view as Launa's psychiatrist, I think it's important to talk about Launa's progress and hopes to come home on an overnight stay. Firstly, if it's okay with you all, I will explain my progress report and my thoughts concerning Launa's new medication and current mental health. Frankie, would Tom and Pip be interested in looking at our toy corner? There are many great games and story books to look and play with."

Dr Linder's suggestion makes me feel more grown up, his obvious diversion for Tom and Pip whilst he talks more in depth, makes me realise the importance of the conversation to come.

"Sure, Tom take Pip over to the toy corner for a while, please."

I notice Mum shifting uncomfortably in her chair, I can't imagine how hard it must be to sit here, to have all this attention focused on you and waiting nervously for a current diagnosis. Dad takes hold of Mum's hand, and Pip, who is sitting on my lap, puts her little palms on to mine and starts to tap them up and down.

"Pip go with your brother for a moment. Look, there is the *Hungry Hippos* game."

Pip slides off my lap reluctantly and heads towards Tom, who is already frantically rummaging through the toys and books that are on offer in the far corner of the room.

"We have as you know placed Launa on a new medication, instead of prescribing Fluoxetine, which is primarily an anti-depressant, the decision was taken to try Seroxat. Now Seroxat is a group of medicines called SSRIs, that stands for Selective, Serotonin Reuptake, Inhibitors. Basically, this drug helps replenish Serotonin levels in the brain. Now, studies have found that people who suffer from depression and anxiety have lower levels of serotonin in their brain. Now the dose prescribed is 40mg, which is to be taken with food first thing in the morning. This medication like most others takes at least two weeks to take effect. Now, Launa, I know we have talked through some of the side affects you are experiencing, as well as the more positive reactions you are experiencing, so I think this is a good opportunity to express any feelings positive or negative you may have with your family here today."

"Well, today so far has been really good, it's so hard to explain how I'm feeling, Doctor. If I could explain it, then I would be home, home where I should be. I've been so excited, so excited about seeing my family today, I have so much I want to say, but I find this hard, really hard."

My mum shifts uncomfortably in her chair, and I sense her agitation.

"Okay, let me put it like this, I understand talking openly in this environment is hard, the point of this meeting together today is to express any feelings that will obviously come up.

"Doctor, is the point, is the real point of this to decide if Launa is ready to come home?"

"It's partly that, Frankie; in my opinion, Launa, you are ready to spend some time at home with your family, that can be a few hours at first, this is what we need to discuss here today."

I find myself slipping in and out of the conversation. I sense the importance of what is being discussed but feel less able to cope with what's being said. I suddenly feel less grown up.

"I want, I need Launa home, I can't spend another day without her." My dad's unexpected words strike me hard like a gunshot heard. I feel in that moment his pain, his absolute personal agony of the past year, his thoughts locked in, disguised, sucked up into his guts, his fatherly protective instincts keeping us safe from these feelings and thoughts, but now they are laid out bare, raw and open.

"I realise your emotions, Frankie, I truly do, it's important to express your thoughts and feelings. I understand that Launa's absence must be very difficult, but can we agree that a slow, even an hourly exposure to home life would be advantageous to you all?"

Dr Linder seems less welcoming all of a sudden, his tone, his demeaner has changed, no happy smile concludes his sentence. My grown-up inclusion in this conversation is beginning to make me feel very uncomfortable.

"I want to go home, I want to read bedtime stories to Pip, I want to listen to Tom explain about the latest game he is playing, I need to talk and spend time with Fran, I need to take long walks with my husband."

"Emotions are high here today, understandably, let's not make any big decisions right now, but let's all try and agree that Launa is near, near to ready to spend some time at home with you all."

Unbelievable! This get-together has just been about a removal opportunity, a pass the buck game. Dr Linder's observations seem to be set in stone, time to move on, time to move out. *I really don't know how to feel about this. I mean, I want, and need Mum home, but not like this, this doesn't feel right, I really don't think we can cope yet.* My back suddenly feels wet again, and I begin to wipe beads of sweat from my forehead then my chin, my heart pounds faster, faster than before, I can taste the disinfectant on my tongue, and I can smell it everywhere.

"Let's take a moment to reflect on the future. As your doctor, I feel really encouraged with your new positive improvement, Launa. Looking through your notes, um, the last cognitive behaviour questionnaire which was taken on Wednesday has you in a very positive place. These questionnaires are a great tool, a great tool for you, and for me. If we look back to when you were first admitted, the scale of your anxiety has improved month by month; the last two months your cognitive therapy scale is in medical terms 'positive'."

Scales, questionnaires, positive improvement, these words seem alien to me; can they not see what I can see? Can these doctors be so naïve? My mum tried to take her life, then in their care she tried again. Ticking a box while under medication surely can't reveal a real diagnosis. I keep my thoughts to myself, biting my lip as to hold it all in, but I know my dad must be itching to speak.

"Look, Dr Linder, I want to spend some time with my family. I can't explain it now… today, but please let me spend some time at home with my family." My mum's voice is unexpected, I felt sure Dad was going to respond to Dr Linder's last comments. The whole room suddenly feels smaller, the walls darker, Tom and Pip sound louder, there is distraction everywhere.

"We want that, Launa, we think that's a good idea; we have talked about this, the meeting today is the first step to realise that."

"Well, great, let's please make a decision then, I can't pussy foot around this anymore Doctor. I want my wife home. Launa, I want you home. If it's for an hour, if it's for two hours at a time, then great, that's what I want, that's what our kids want."

My dad's tone is raised, almost high pitched, I know that voice, that voice is angry; some people go silent, some people shout, my dad looks like he is going to cry, that's when I know my dad is angry.

"So, where do we go from here? I mean here now, what happens next? To be honest, Doctor, I want Launa home now, now this minute?"

"Frankie… love, calm down, please calm down; the kids."

"The kids, the kids, that's all I can think about, Launa, they need you, love, I need you."

If Dr Linder's objective was to get my mum and dad speaking honestly then he is succeeding. The passion, the emotion between them is being laid out bare in this magnolia cell. I hold back my own tears as I appreciate and recognise the honesty being spoken.

"Frankie, Launa, Fran; that's not going to happen today, the idea behind this meeting today is to discuss when that can happen. I suggest that a home visit next Saturday would be the best starting point."

"What, next week, why? Why not now, what's going to change in a week?" My dad is now leaning forward in his chair, leaning ever closer to Dr Linder; I resist the urge to grab my dad's arm and pull him back, "Why not now, why not, Doctor?"

"Please, please, Frankie, just listen. Next week is fine, I can do that, I look forward to that, I want to do that." My mum's words seem to work. My Dad, tight and tense a second ago, seems to relent. He slowly rests his large back into the cloth covered chair, sighing loudly as his head rests against the back.

"Okay, let's conclude then by saying that Launa is ready to spend some time at home. I suggested next Saturday because I feel that having Fran and Tom home, and not at school, would be the best environment for Launa to return to. We can plan today the timing, the logistics if you will, now that we are all together. Frankie, I know you work long hours, you have mentioned that before."

"I work long hours to keep busy, Doctor, I work to forget, I don't work to live."

"Okay, that's hard, and you are doing so well, Frankie, your children are happy, and healthy, that's a credit to you both. Can we plan a time and date for you both next Saturday?"

It has come, it's here, the day ahead feels heavy, the week is going to feel long, painfully long. I knew this day was coming, I didn't think it was going to feel like this though. I pictured a fluffy, sunlit day; my mum would walk through our garden gate, holding her travel bag over her shoulder, with a beaming smile and maybe a gift for us all.

The next minutes pass me by without actually involving me, like a vivid dream, my actual presence is not needed. I see Dad signing some paperwork, I notice Mum's face, it looks drawn, it seems grey and aged.

"Fran, can you grab the kids, we are heading off soon? Fran, get the kids!"

My head is dull, my dad's words seem distant, not meant for me. "Sure, okay, Dad, are we heading home, can we go home now, Dad?"

Leaving is always hard, always emotional, but today the hugs and kisses feel forced, especially between Mum and me. Pip doesn't want to let go of Mum's arm and Tom, well, Tom has said his goodbyes and is already heading towards the car.

The meeting with Dr Linder had, I think, been awkward for all of us. Mum's decision to say yes to coming home next Saturday felt forced, the decision was already made for her. I mean, what else was she going to say with all that focus on her?

"Right, come on, Pip, say your goodbyes; Mummy is coming home next Saturday, it's so exciting, isn't it? Let's leave Mum to rest, we can go home and plan for a lovely day ahead for all of us." I take hold of Pip's little arms and repeat my goodbyes to Mum.

"Okay, love, you have a good week, I look forward to coming home for a few hours. We could have a nice walk together."

"Sounds good, Mum." I carry Pip over the grey gravel car park and leave Dad to say his goodbyes.

"Oh, Frankie, that was hard. This new medication is definitely working though. A few weeks ago, that meeting, I mean the thought of having a meeting would have had me anxious in anticipation all week."

"I know, love, I think it went well. We had to talk like that, we needed to hear from Dr Linder, he seems positive about you, doesn't he?"

"Yeah, he does. The kids look really well, love; it's been a tiring few hours, I am going to have a rest now, maybe have a relaxing bath. Give me a text when you are home, and let's talk throughout the week."

"Okay, my love, we will get there you know, all of us will get there."

I finish buckling up Pip in her car seat and take my seat. Dad gives a final wave and heads towards the driver's door. My dad lowers himself into his seat and gives out a big sigh, he rubs his hair, then shakes his head as if to clear his thoughts. "Well, little ones, we okay?" He doesn't leave any pause before continuing. "It's good news, isn't it? I know it's hard to see your mum in this place, but things are moving forward. Mum is coming home, maybe not for the night, but it's a start, it's a beginning."

I can see the excitement in my dad's eyes, he seems looser somehow, his face is less sullen, that constant frown has lessened. The journey home is above all a quiet one. My dad tries to get us all talking, but apart from Tom reminding us all of his plans to meet Noah at the park, and Pip playing patter cake with me, the short car ride home is quiet and non-eventful.

"Right, its dinner time, how about a baguette from the Spar? We could have those three-cheese ones?"

"Yeah, can I have a packet of cheese and onion squares as well, Dad?"

"Why not. Fran, you want some crisps too?"

"No, a baguette will be enough thanks. Get Pip a sausage roll, Dad, and a Fruit Shoot, please."

"Was planning to, love, I am all over it."

Food bought; we make our way home. My message tone sounds and its Tanya, who else? "u ok F, look lets catch up l8tr, Teddys got a bottle of vodka, and some other treats! Luvs u T, txt me xxx."

I resist the temptation to reply straight away. The thought of meeting Tanya makes me happy, though. I feel a bit reckless; a drink sounds good. I've had vodka before; Tanya had nicked a small bottle from her dad's drinks cabinet. We both took turns to swig it down at the park. It was fun until Tanya had thrown up all over herself. We had to sneak back to mine to clean her up. Luckily my dad was at the Fountain, and Aunty Pam was busy in the front room keeping Pip entertained. In fact, I never got that hooded top back from her.

Anyway, we pull up outside our house and Tom grabs the Spar bag as I manoeuvre Pip out of her car seat.

"Come on, kids. Let's plate up our dinner. Tom, you can make us all a squash."

"Oh, Dad, why me?"

"Because I asked you, and Fran is busy with Pip, that's why."

It's strange, the morning spent with Mum seems forgotten. Tom and Dad are demolishing their three-cheese baguettes whilst watching *Match of the Day*, Pip is chewing on her sausage roll in her baby bouncer chair, and I am sitting on one of our kitchen stools slowly eating my baguette whilst staring out of our kitchen window at the children playing in the gardens opposite.

I don't know how to feel, I guess I expected things to feel a little different, but the everyday keeps moving forward, doesn't it? My morning has left me feeling confused, worn out and uncertain of what happens next. I decide in that moment to reply to Tanya and plan our catch-up later, a drink with her and Teddy is going to be fun; I talk to myself; I convince myself into it, I need some fun today.

"Lovely, that hit the spot. Aunty Pam is coming over about three-ish; Tom, you are meeting Noah down the park, what time again?"

"Four o'clock, Dad, we are going to play football and then play some *Call of Duty* back here."

"Great, Fran, what's your plans?"

"I am going to have a bath, and then meet Tanya in town."

"Okay, what time love?"

"About five, we are going to get some popcorn and then walk back to hers and watch some DVDs."

"Nice. I am heading to the rugby club later, say four-ish, have a couple of pints with Johnno and the boys. Pam is going to baby sit Pip for a few hours, okay?"

"Yeah, great, Dad, what time are you coming home?"

"Well, Pam hasn't got any plans, so we will see, love."

I know what that means. I mean, I understand my dad needs some time out, time to relax, but if Pam is willing, my Dad will stay out for hours; the thought of that makes my stomach turn over again. Is he going to drink too much? Is he going to keep it together after today? God, I can't stop worrying, I take a huge swallow which almost makes me retch, my mouth tastes bitter, and my head begins to hurt.

I spend the next hour or so tidying up the kitchen then hoovering my bedroom. Dad and Tom are engrossed with the FA Cup being played out on the TV. Pip is sleeping, she always does after food, her sweet little face produces sleep smiles, they are so cute; her chubby arms are, as always, resting gently on her pot belly. Whilst putting the dishes away I notice Dad has opened a Strongbow; I can't help but feel a little concerned, when my dad drinks, he drinks. He doesn't drink that often. I mean during the week, he's up working by five thirty, normally in bed by nine, but when he drinks, he drinks. I feel uneasy, why is it down to me to see the negative, I am only fifteen, not fifty?

Three o'clock slowly comes around. I've taken my bath and Dad is finishing his third can when the door is knocked.

"Come in, Pam, Pam come in, your sister is coming home!"

I feel embarrassed if I am honest. Aunty Pam deserves a little one to one, not my Dad's raised cider speak from his front room chair.

"Great Frankie, I did speak to Launa earlier, love, she is so excited about next Saturday, a bit tired I think, but really excited about next week. Hello, little Pip, how are you, my love? Oh, Frankie, that smile gets me every time. Fran, you okay?"

"Not bad, Aunty, it's been a strange day. Mum looks well. Mum is coming home for a few hours next Saturday. I am sure she has explained all of that if you have spoken to her earlier."

"She has, love, I think it's fantastic; Tom, you excited with that news?"

"Can't wait Aunty Pam, it's going to be a good Saturday, isn't it?"

"It will, love, your mum is so excited. We could take a walk on the moor, maybe head to Haytor if it is dry."

"Yeah, Haytor. I love climbing the big rocks up there."

"I know you do, Tom, let's see when Saturday comes around. Right then, what's everyone's plans for this afternoon? Fran what you up to?"

"Catching up with Tanya, about five-ish, going to meet her outside the Spar."

"Okay, lovely, and what about you, Tom?"

"Playing footie with Noah at the park, going to meet him down there say four-ish, and then coming home to play some Xbox."

"Great, have you all had your lunch?"

"Yes, Pam, they are all fed and watered. I am going to grab a quick shower, and then head down to the Rugby Club."

"Okay, that's good. Frankie, don't think you've got to rush home, I've got nowhere to be; and Fran, you staying over at Tanya's?"

That's a good question, I think to myself. "Was hoping to; is that all right, Dad?" My dad is swigging his third can, whilst chucking his empties into the kitchen bin.

"That's fine, as long as Tanya's parents don't mind?"

"I'll text her now." I pick up my phone, but instead of texting Tanya, I turn my attention towards little Pip.

Pip, bless her, has slept through all of this chatter, and now I notice she has buried her face into the side of her bouncer chair, one leg is sticking out with her sock half off her little foot. Both her chubby arms are resting either side of the chair.

I don't text Tanya straight away, because I already know I can stay at hers, I just wanted to leave my options open. *Let's see how tonight goes,* I think to myself. I may need to come home, who knows? I can't really think straight at the moment.

The expectation, the past memories of getting drunk with Tanya, the vodka, and its effects, that warm feeling inside and having a real giggle with her and Teddy is the only thing on my mind. I leave everyone downstairs and head to my bedroom to sort out my clothes for later.

"Right, I am off for that shower; Pam, help yourself to anything."

"Will do, I'll make a cuppa in a moment."

"Aunty Pam, could I please put my Xbox on for half an hour… please?"

"Well, okay, Tom, but just for a little bit. Keep the volume down, I think when Pip wakes up, I may take her for a little walk."

"Thanks, Aunty, I'll play with my headphones on, then there will be no noise."

***

I hear Dad start the shower and then pull the shower curtain across. I take a seat on the edge of my bed and decide to reply to Tanya. Her last message mentioned, "and other treats". I wonder what she meant by that. Maybe another kind of drink, some fags or I remember her talking about Jägermeister before. She and Jenna Hardwick had got drunk on it one Saturday after Tanya had a huge row with her mum over what she was wearing that day. Jenna had supplied the booze, and Tanya had nicked some fags from her dad's duty frees which he had brought back from their family holiday to Benidorm. I was visiting Mum that Saturday and remember receiving drunken texts with random, blurry pictures all throughout the day.

I write a text to Tanya and touch send on my phone. *"Hi T, looking 4ward to cing u, Wots other treats? xx"*

Tanya replies almost instantly, "Lol, u will like them, it's a surprise m8, cu at 5 by the spar, luvs u."

Interesting, Tanya normally wouldn't be able to resist telling me. My imagination wonders, what is it?

I hear the bathroom door open and listen to my dad's footsteps as he heads towards his bedroom.

"You finished in the bathroom, Dad?"

"Yes, all done love."

I am keen to get ready, my stomach is full of excitement, unlike earlier when these sensations made my stomach feel sick. Now, I feel different, I feel excited, a little nervous too, but it's a nice feeling. I grab my underwear and head to the bathroom. The floor is soaking wet, my dad always leaves a puddle. I don't understand where all the water comes from, surely, he can stand on a towel while drying himself? Anyway, I pop a spare towel on to the floor and start to undress for my shower.

***

"Tom, Tom… Tom! you fancy a squash or something?"

"Oh, sorry I didn't hear you; no, I am fine, Aunty. It looks like Pip is waking up."

"Okay, love, I'll let her come around a bit first, you heading off to the park soon?"

"Yeah, what time is it please?"

"Quarter to four, love."

"Okay, I'll just finish this game and then head out."

***

"Ah, that's better, I feel refreshed now, it's amazing what a Strongbow and a hot shower can do for you. Oh, hello, sleepy head, you okay my little orange Pip?"

"Da, da, gone sleeping."

"I know, love, your big belly was full, and you fell fast asleep."

"She's growing up so much, Frankie. I mean it only seems like yesterday when she first started talking, remember she was quite slow with her speech at first, she's getting there now though."

"Definitely, she is. We were all a little worried at first, but hey, all babies are different. I think Fran was talking when she came out of the womb! And Tom, well Tom was asking for chocolate cake at six months."

"Ha-ha, they are all doing so well, love, Launa must see that she must take comfort knowing her children are doing so well. I mean they are just so content."

"Thanks, Pam, that means a lot, you have a great deal to do with that, you know, I don't know where we would be without your help, the kids love having you around."

"Well, it's my pleasure, Frankie, I love being around them all. Things are moving, really moving forward, aren't they? Launa coming home for a few hours next Saturday; Fran getting stuck into her swimming; Tom getting out and about, making new friends and socialising; and Pip, well her smiling face, her expressions, she is turning into a right little character."

"Things feel more positive, Pam, it's going to take some working on, I know, when Launa comes home. But with all the things we have all gone through, the struggles, the emotional rollercoaster ride, it has got to be worth it. Launa seems to be ready, she wants to come home, we all have to be here for her. I can't wait, I really can't wait for next Saturday."

"Dad, Dad, can I have a pound, to get a drink after playing footie, please?"

"Hold on a minute, Tom, can't you see I am talking to, Aunty Pam?"

"It's okay, Frankie, we can talk more later if you want. I am going to get Pip ready anyway and then head out for a little walk."

"Okay, I'll be heading out soon, too. I'll wait for Fran to get out of the bathroom and say goodbye. Tom, catch, I've only got a two-pound coin, so treat yourself."

"Cool, thanks, Dad."

***

I use my favourite Molton Brown shampoo, it always makes my hair feel really shiny and full. The shampoo makes my hair smell like citrus fruits. I got it as a gift set, it was a Christmas present from my dad last year and I knew it cost more than he could really afford. It's my going out, my best going out shampoo.

I slip on my clean underwear and start applying my body moisturiser. It's funny isn't it, the routines that become instinctive, every day, almost done without any real thought or consciousness. I don't really feel clean, even after a shower, until I've applied my daily moisturiser; it smells of coconuts, I love the feeling of it on my skin, I love the smell of it too.

"Fran, you out the shower? I am heading off soon?... Your brother, Pam and Pip are nearly ready to leave as well."

"Just finishing up in the bathroom, Dad, you go if you are ready, I'll be fine."

"Yeah, I know, love, but I need to know if it's okay for you to stay at Tanya's, remember?"

"It's fine, Dad, I just heard back from her, we are going to watch some DVDs and spend a girly night together."

"Okay, just let me know what time you are planning to come back in the morning. Love you, have a good night."

"Will do, you too, text you in the morning."

The question now of leaving my options open has been closed, whatever happens later, I'll need to be able to stay at Tanya's. That really doesn't bother me, the thought of where I stay seems a far-off, unimportant detail right now. The overriding thought right now is that for at least half an hour,

our house is going to be empty, empty and quiet, that doesn't happen that often.

"Right, we are all off, Fran, any change of plans, just let me and Pam know, please."

"Yes, Dad! Will do, just go and enjoy your drink with Johnno and the others."

"Okay, bye, love."

I can overhear their muffled voices in the hallway, I recognise Tom's voice, a high-pitched tone, chatting instead of just putting on his jacket. I imagine Pam fretting, making sure she has everything Pip needs for their mammoth twenty-minute walk together. I hear Dad's voice as he tries to manoeuvre them all politely and quickly out of the front door.

The door finally slams shut, and for a few seconds I just shut my eyes, take a deep breath and think of nothing in particular.

I open my chest of drawers and rifle through the untidy array of T-shirts and tops I have dumped inside; I've never put my tops in any particular order. My chest of drawers has always been a bit of a jumble sale mess. I choose a black, long sleeve top, as wearing black always looks good on me. The top looks a little crumpled, but I am going to wear my favourite Hollister hoody over the top, so that doesn't really matter; who's going to see it anyway?

I take a look at my small collection of perfumes and sprays sitting on my chest of drawers. My mum's favourite perfume is Chanel No 5. My choices are cheap in comparison, perfumes brought for me as a birthday or Christmas present.

The first time I crept into my mum and dad's room to sneak a spray of Mum's expensive perfume was not long after her committal to Park Place. I remember feeling a pang of excitement, mixed with a little guilt. I was catching up with Tanya and a few other friends later on that day, and for some reason felt the need to smell different, expensive, maybe I just needed to smell Mum's smell again.

Dad, Tom and Pip were downstairs, and I remember tiptoeing over Mum and Dad's wooden floorboards; every creek and squeak seemed amplified, I held my breath as if to stay silent. When I reached my mum's dresser, I slowly, deliberately picked up her favourite perfume. It felt heavy in my hands, the glass bottle, square in design was over half full of its light brown liquid.

I nervously looked for the spray hole, I then panicked, and totally over sprayed the scent all over my left shoulder. I tried spraying it again, and then remembered watching women on TV and films, they would spray the scent onto their wrist, and then rub them both together. I did that, I tried that not really knowing why I was doing it. I left my parents' bedroom that day feeling very guilty, feeling that I had done something very naughty, something so wrong.

My mum's perfume collection still sits on her dresser, alongside her make-up, hairbrushes and other cosmetics. I have never used any of her stuff since that day.

I spray a little of my Beyonce Heat perfume on to my neck and across my chest, then as I always do since that day, give my right wrist a little spray, which I rub instinctively onto my left without fail.

Our house is silent, I can hear small children playing on our street, I can hear people mowing their lawns, I can hear sports being played out on distant TVs. These sounds are comforting to me, they allow me to just take a moment, a moment to myself.

Jeans, jeans would be best I decide. I have a great pair of skinny jeans that have been my favourite for the past couple of months now, they feel so comfortable, they fit nice and show off my athletic long legs and firm bum.

When I do the washing, I always grab my favourite jeans out first. Then I put them out to dry on my bedroom radiator, they are just the best, you know what I mean? Comfortable, fitted, they make you feel great, you just know you look good in them.

I slip on my jeans and tuck my black top into the waist. I leave my belt unbuckled as I concentrate on my make-up, I hate the feeling of being belt ready before I've put my makeup on. My make-up routine for school is quick and simple; concealer, a little neutral-coloured lipstick, maybe some eyeliner. This afternoon I have more time, my time, a lot more time to pamper myself, a chance to even apply a little red lipstick to finish.

Using my stand-up mirror, I take a look at myself; this mirror is kind to me, I mean every mirror seems to portray a different you, don't you think? When I am at school for example, the girl's toilet mirror is less than flattering, it reflects back, a wide ever expanding me. My legs look fat, my face seems round like a football.

My message tone sounds. "U nearly ready F? If so, I am heading to the Spar, can u bring some booze? Xxx"

"Only my Dads cider, he'll kill me though! Xxx"

"don't worry then m8, u got cash for food l8tr?"

"Food? I haven't thought about food xx"

"Don't worry, u won't want much of a munch after your goodies, just bring yourself bitch, Lol xx"

"Goodies"? What is she talking about? Tanya's texts aren't making a lot of sense, is she playing a game, it wouldn't be the first time?

"I can't bring BOZ T, I've only got £5 on me, wots the plan? Xxx"

"The plan is you get your skinny ass over to the spar asap; Teddy and Robbie are waiting xxx"

Robbie, Robbie Stokes, Teddy's best mate. I knew it, I felt something different was going on. I know Robbie, of course I do, spending most of my time with Tanya means getting to know Teddy, then after a while, Teddy's friends. I've only met Robbie a couple of times, but never have really spoken to him, he seemed a bit quiet the first time I met him, a little shy even.

What is Tanya up to? This is beginning to feel like a bad idea. What has she said to Teddy and Robbie?

I take a moment, just to think and then decide, I am going to go anyway, it's going to be fun. I finish my make-up, take one last look at myself in the mirror. I do my belt up and slip on my best trainers.

Downstairs, I grab a can of Dad's cider out of the fridge without really thinking about it. I do feel a bit nervous; I open the can and start to swallow big swigs of the sweet fizzy liquid; it burns my throat at first. On the third big gulp I begin to cough, the fizz goes up my nose and I struggle to keep the cider inside my mouth.

The cold can in my hand suddenly seems to hold too much liquid for me. I take a deep breath and start swigging it again. *When I finish it, I will crush the can and chuck it in the bin at the end of our street.*

For a moment, I think I hear Aunty Pam's voice, in that split second, I freeze, I don't move a muscle, I just listen, listen closely. The sound of a woman's voice disappears, it must have just been from the houses over the road or someone just walking by.

Still feeling a little panicked I empty the rest of the can down the kitchen sink, I've had enough anyway. I stamp on the empty can and slip it into my hoody pocket.

"On my way T. Wot u planning crazy? Xx"

"Fun, fun you need it, cu soon M8 lol xxx"

I lock the front door behind me and head out, the early summer sun hits my eyes, I squint as I grab for my sunglasses, the warmth feels nice, maybe I shouldn't have worn this hoody.

The walk into town is only ten minutes at most, but I find myself rushing, like some overexcited kid.

Taking a right on to Maple Drive, I look up and see Aunty Pam and Pip heading towards me up the hill.

"Hi, love, you look nice, off to meet Tanya?"

"Oh, yeah, thanks, Aunty, meeting her now, you had a nice walk with little Pip?"

I really don't want to get into a long conversation here, I swallow hard and hope Aunty Pam can't smell my cider breath.

"Yeah, it was a nice, just a little wander, we just popped down to the park. Tom was there, having a kick around with Noah and a few of the other boys."

"Great, I'll give Pip a kiss and head off, Tanya is already waiting."

"Okay, you have a good time, love."

Kiss given; I continue my march towards the Spar.

As the Spar comes into view, I see Tanya leaning on the small shopping trolleys parked outside.

"Fran! Fran!" Tanya shouts, "I am so excited to see you, you're looking lovely, you skinny bitch."

Tanya comes running towards me, I mean running fast, her arms and legs are pumping up and down. She looks like a sprinter, stretching every muscle to win a race.

"Wow, Tan, you okay? What's happening?"

"I loves you; I am just so happy to see you; Teddy and Robbie are just in the Spar getting a bottle of Coke."

"Cool, I couldn't get any booze though, Tan, I drank a can of my Dad's cider earlier, aw, it was awful; fizzy and sweet, I couldn't finish it."

"Nutter, cider is shit. We've got vodka, strong vodka from Teddy's house."

"You had some already? You seem all over the place."

"Well, maybe I am, but it's not the vodka, don't hate me, it's the Benzo Fury."

"Benzo Fury, what that powder stuff, that legal high drug, the one that's in the news?"

"Yeah, but it's okay, it's nice, it makes you feel nice, I am off my tits, I've only had a little line, and I'm buzzing. Teddy got it off Robbie; we all had a line each in my bedroom."

"Aw, I don't know, Tan, I've never tried anything like that before."

"You'll love it, babe, honestly, you deserve a break, you know with all that stuff with your mum to deal with. I'll look after you."

"How do you take it? Does it hurt?"

"No, crazy; you just snort it up your nose, just try a little bit like me, it doesn't hurt, it tastes bitter, but that's all."

"Where, where can I do it?"

"When they both come out the shop, we can head to the park, you know where I mean, the fields after the footie pitch, no one ever goes down there."

"Bloody hell, Tan, what have you said to Robbie? I've never even spoken to him, it's going to feel really weird, like you have set us both up on a blind date or something."

"No way, he's cute, I just wanted you to come out, come on, no promises, just have a laugh, have a drink, we can always head home when we want to."

Shit, I want to try it, I really want to have a drink and a laugh. My head is in a spin though, I've heard about this Benzo Fury stuff before, but never knew Tanya was into it. Maybe its Teddy, has he got Tanya into that kind of stuff?

"Okay, what's taking them so long? Can we take the lower path, Tanya? Tom is at the park with his mates, I don't want him to see me, you know, because he'll tell Dad."

"Yeah, of course, we'll take the lower path. Fran, honestly you'll love it, it makes me want to just dance, or run, I am so full of energy, I want to just drink, drink all day long."

Tanya sees Teddy slowly coming out of the Spar.

"Teddy, bloody hell, me and Fran thought you were arrested for shop lifting or something."

"Never catch me, babe, no, there was a massive old people queue. Robbie was freaking out, I thought he was going to faint at one point."

"Very funny, Ted, you had to wipe the sweat from your head, your eyes look massive, mate."

"Nice try, Robbie, I am all over this stuff, come on, let's head off."

"Follow us, boys, if you dare! Come on, Fran, let's get going; boys always follow, that's the rules."

Tanya takes my arm, like a parent might do when you are out on a family walk. We both skip along together on the pavement as we leave Teddy and Robbie slowly walking behind us.

For the first time in ages, I begin to feel a sense of freedom, just skipping down this pavement with Tanya, I start to feel a lightening, a loosening of tension all over my body, friends are so important, Tanya is such a good friend.

"Come on, slackers, catch up. Me and Fran are so fast."

I am fast, but I don't know if I can keep up with this hyperactive acting Tanya. We skirt around the park's sports fields, taking the well-worn path that dog walkers take on their daily stroll. I glance over at the football pitch, I don't make out Tom, but see that there is a kickabout going on in the distance.

"Fran, let's wait for Teddy and Robbie here; we could sit on the bank, I fancy a drink now, don't you?"

"Can do, are we going to have some of that Benzo Fury stuff as well?"

"You want too? Teddy's got it; we could have a go when he gets here."

"Yeah, let's do it, you promise to look after me though."

"Of course, mate, I am your besties friend. I've already told my mum that you are staying with me tonight. Just give it go, we've got the vodka, and now we've got the Benzo Fury!"

"Okay, okay, let's wait for them here then."

"Cool, take seat, they won't be long.

"Oh yes, Fran, it's going to be so good, I am so glad you came out. Teddy has a straw, that's how you take it, you just put a bit of powder on a flat surface, like the back of your phone. Anyway, have a swig of that while we wait, it's so strong, I've brought an empty bottle so we can mix it with the Coke, but just have it neat for now."

I take a small sip. "Ah, bloody hell, Tan, that's so strong."

"I know, its black label or something, it's the strongest you can get."

Teddy and Robbie finally catch up with us.

"You two started drinking it already? I thought you wanted to mix it with the Coke."

"We couldn't wait, Teddy, you and Robbie are such slow walkers; me and Fran are hardcore."

"Hardcore, ha-ha. You want hardcore, take a big gulp then, not a little girly sip."

Tanya does just that, she takes a huge gulp, swallows hard and then gives out a loud cough. I take a gulp, but it's not as big as Tanya's. I can feel the vodka hitting my stomach, it feels warm then really hot, my throat starts to burn.

"Okay, now you two have a go, me and Fran have had big gulps; and no little boy sips, we want to see big manly gulps."

Teddy takes the bottle from me. "Bottoms up," he says as he takes a huge gulp, swallows that and then takes another. "Come on!" he shouts out loud.

"Your turn, Robbie, match that, mate."

He does, but on his second gulp, chokes and has to spit out most of the neat vodka.

"Bloody hell, mate, that's a waste, what a pussy."

Robbie doesn't reply, he carries on coughing, and for one moment looks like he is going to throw up. Tanya and Teddy fall about laughing. I give out a little giggle but in truth feel a bit sorry for Robbie as he continues to cough and choke out loud.

"Right, lets mix the rest, we can't have Robbie wasting it all, can we?"

"Yeah, that's true, pass me the empty bottle, Tanya."

Teddy pours the vodka, then the Coke into the bottle, a lot of vodka, a little Coke, the liquid looks thin, only slightly browned by the amount of Coke he's added.

"Teddy, get that powder out, let's have a little line here, we can do it off the back of my phone if you want?"

"Cool, Fran should go first, she's got some catching up to do!"

"Fran, you happy to go first?"

"Yeah, yeah, I think so, what have I got to do?"

"I tell you what, watch me, it's easy."

Tanya takes the small see-through bag off Teddy and empties some powder on to the back of her phone. She uses Teddy's plastic credit card to crush and chop up the powder.

"Right, I've put it into two lines, watch me, Fran."

Tanya, snorts hard, using the straw to take it up her right nostril.

"Wow, that felt like a big one."

"What does it do, how does it make you feel?"

"It makes you feel warm all over, you'll have so much energy, Fran, me and Robbie do it all the time. Tanya's just getting into it, but she loves it."

I feel excited, nervous and pressured into giving it a go. I never knew Tanya was into this sort of thing. I take the straw and put it up my right nostril.

"I'll hold the phone, Fran, you just snort when you are ready."

I snort, the instant sensation is a stinging up my nose, then I get a bitter taste in the back of my throat.

"Really snort it back, Fran, swallow hard."

I do just that, but after swallowing hard my first reaction is to retch, I hold back the sick, I don't want to make a fool of myself, so I concentrate on just holding the bitter, sicky taste in my mouth. After a few seconds, the retching eases. I take another swallow, and then start having a tingling sensation that rises from the back of my neck and up towards the top of my head, when it reaches my forehead I begin to feel lightheaded.

"Well done, mate, you did it like pro, feels nice, doesn't it?"

"Yeah… it does, I've got a tingly sensation all over me, especially in my head."

I watch Teddy and Robbie take their lines, they do it quickly and with ease. I do feel nice, my stomach is full of butterflies, but unlike earlier it feels good. My legs feel full of energy, not heavy and tired.

We all decide to head further down the path. Once you get past the sports fields you end up in a farmer's field. From there you can take another path that leads you down towards the riverbank, we walk fast, all of us talking, talking about everything and anything.

We reach the riverbank and then step down onto the stony edge of the riverbed. It is dry, so we all take a seat, and start passing the vodka and coke around.

"I love this, Tan, I really needed this, it's been a weird time, you know with my mum and all that. But this is a great idea."

"I knew it, I knew you would enjoy it, I didn't mention the Benzo Fury powder, because at first I thought you might hate me for it."

"No way, I'll never hate you, you are my best friend, best friend forever."

Me and Tanya have a hug, a long tight close hug. It's strange, I don't know if it's this Benzo stuff, but me and Tanya have really connected again. We are into each other again, and the apprehension of earlier, I mean having Robbie here, and not knowing how the evening was going to go, those worries, and doubts have disappeared.

Teddy and Robbie start skimming stones down along the shallow river, boys make a game of everything.

"That was a sixer, beat that, bro."

"Easy, watch this."

"Total fail, bro, that wasn't even a oner."

"Girls, give this a go, Teddy can't even get a twoer."

"No, you're all right, me and Fran are drinking anyway. Let's have a bit more of that stuff, shall we?"

"Bloody hell, Tan, give me a minute, greedy."

"Greedy! No, hardcore, love!"

"'Love', okay, I enjoyed you saying that… catch this."

Tanya completely misses her catch, and stumbles forward to quickly pick up the little bag from the dry, stony floor.

"Good catch, love, stick to swimming I would, I don't think netball's going to be your game."

We all laugh; laugh out loud. Teddy is funny, he has a wicked sense of humour, quick, and sarcastic.

"Yeah, don't try tennis either, your hand-eye coordination is shit." Robbie isn't as funny as Teddy.

The second line goes down easier than the first; I've joined the club, I've become a member, I think to myself.

***

Two hours have passed, and we haven't really moved from the riverside. The vodka has been mixed again and again. We've just sat around on this dry riverbed like you might around a campfire. I can't stop talking; it feels to me like I am having the most important conversation I am ever going to have.

With the amount of vodka, we've drunk I expected to feel pissed by now. But far from it, my head feels full, I mean full of thoughts, I can't speak those thoughts quick enough. Before when I've had a drink, my head starts to feel thick, dizzy, my thoughts would then turn to food, but not today, my body needs more drink, not fish 'n' chips or chocolate cake.

"I've got to go pee, it's okay for you two boys, but I am not going to go outside, I've got to pee."

"Yeah, I could do with a pee as well, Tanya. Can we go to the leisure centre, use theirs?"

"Just go behind a bush both of you."

"No way, I need toilet paper."

"Yeah, me too, come on, let's go."

After some huffing and puffing from the boys, we all get to our feet. As soon as I stand, my head spins, my heart races, my legs suddenly don't belong to me!

"Wow, that's a rush, I forgot that feeling when you stand up quickly and the blood seems to rush through you."

"You okay, Fran?"

"I think so, got a dizzy feeling though, my legs feel numb."

"Just shake them out, we've been sitting for so long, just move about a bit. You'll see, when we start walking it will feel better."

Tanya is right, once I've started to move around a little bit, my dizziness disappears, and that nice warm feeling returns. In fact, once we start to walk, I feel a rush of energy from somewhere deep inside.

Tanya now takes my arm again, and I can smell cigarettes on her breath and wonder if she can smell the same on mine. The leisure centre is only a short walk away from the sports fields. It's dangerously close to the rugby club where my dad will be, but it's closer and easier to get to than heading to mine, and also, I couldn't face Aunty Pam, right now.

"You feeling okay, Franny?"

"Yeah, feeling good, that's the first time you have called me Franny for a while."

"Well, it's your name, mate, I just wanted you to know I am here for you, that's all."

"Oh, thanks, babe, appreciate that, what are we going to do after this?"

"Well it's still light, shall we pop into town, see who's around the clock tower?"

"Really? I don't fancy doing that, I am just happy being around you, Teddy and Robbie, I don't want to see anyone else, Tan."

"Okay, we could head up to the bus shelter, have a bit more of that? Then later head back down to the fields, maybe."

"Nice, yeah, can we do that?"

"Defo, let's just get to the toilet, I am busting."

We retake our earlier steps along the lower path, and then past the sports fields.

Again, I glance over towards the football pitch, this time though the pitch looks empty, all I can make out is a couple of people taking their dogs out for a walk.

My mouth feels dry, so I pop a stick of juicy fruit into my mouth and offer Tanya one.

"Yeah, love one; boys, you want a chewy?"

"No thanks, we've got fags going, maybe in a bit."

We skirt around the two rugby pitches to our left, and then take a wide berth past the actual rugby clubhouse. I can't imagine seeing my dad when I am in this state. I have a flutter of nerves deep in my belly as the path takes us in view of the rugby club.

The leisure centre is further along again, past the rugby pitches and household recycling centre. It's an old, grey, concrete building with a gym, squash and badminton courts. Outside is a small play area, with climbing frames and swings; next to that there is one tarmac tennis court and five a side football pitch.

We reach the car park, which is full, and me and Tanya push open the large glass doors which lead to the reception and toilets. As soon as I am through the doors, my vision starts to go blurry, I notice the sounds of children using the vending machines, I can even hear the coins dropping, everything seems louder than normal, I feel panicked, hot and awkward, sweat forms on my forehead, and I feel off balance.

"Fran, Fran, you okay?"

"Not sure, let's just use the toilet and get out of here."

"Sure, come on then, you'll be fine once we are out in the fresh air again."

I find it hard to concentrate on using the toilet, the pale blue, graffiti-covered cubicle feels so much smaller than I can remember. The noises of the leisure centre, the coming and going of people, seem to echo straight through me. I can feel every sound in my chest, my head is full of sounds, and my ears are ringing.

"Come on, Fran, I am done, shall I wait outside for you?"

"I can't pee, Tan, I can't seem to relax."

"Oh, mate, just breathe, it took me a while to go too."

"Okay, okay, just wait outside, outside in the reception, please."

"Will do, no rush."

I hear the toilet door shutting as Tanya leaves. The sweat is now streaming down my back, I pull some toilet paper off the roll and use it to wipe my neck and face. The cubicle smells, and then I have a horrible thought, is it me that is smelling? I smell my armpits, and then smell them again, it's hard to tell where the smell is coming from. I swallow hard and can taste the smell in my mouth. *Is it my breath?* I think to myself.

The fun and rush from earlier, the nice warm feelings and thoughts I experienced just minutes ago seem to have just disappeared. Now, I feel in a right state, I manage to pee a little and then quickly pull up my jeans. I've just got to get out of this smelly, small cubicle.

I take a look at myself in the toilet mirror, my skin looks pale and my pupils are wide and black. I splash lots of cold water onto my face and then try to tidy up my hair. "Right, I am ready." I shake my head as if to clear my mind, then quickly head out of the door.

Once in the busy reception area my eyes quickly look for Tanya. I panic when I don't see her at first, it seems like everyone's looking at me, I frantically look around again and finally see Tanya standing by one of the tall glass windows.

"Fran, over here."

"Do I look awful, Tan? I feel really strange."

"You look fine, honestly, you are just having a moment. I've felt a bit weird after taking this stuff before, but you'll be fine. Come on, let's just get outside, the boys will be wondering where we've got to."

Teddy and Robbie are sitting on the grass bank, which is opposite the main car park.

"Bloody hell, where have you been, you two? I know girls like to go to the toilet together but me and Robbie thought you had decided to have a workout in the gym!"

"Very funny, Teddy, no, we just needed some time to make us look beautiful again."

"Well it hasn't worked."

"Shut up, Teddy."

"What's the plan then, girls? We haven't got much vodka left. We could head to mine, get some more, my mum and dad are out having a meal up at the golf club."

"I thought we planned to go up to the bus shelter? Me and Fran fancy another line of that."

"We could do that at mine, get some booze and then head back out."

"Fran, you happy to do that?"

I can't make any decisions, I think to myself, my sweating has stopped though, and being outside has definitely helped.

"Yeah, could do, can we go back to the river though after?"

Everyone seems to agree to that, so we head out of the leisure centre car park and start walking up to Teddy's house.

His house stands alone at the top of Tawton Heights. It's a large white building with a garage and a big garden. From his house you can look down and see the whole of the town. In the night you can make out the house because of its bright patio and garden nightlights.

"Mate, is your dad not going to notice his booze is missing?"

"Well, not straight away, no. He keeps boxes of the stuff in the garage, especially vodka. He buys it in bulk, off some dodgy bloke, he reckons he saves loads of money doing it that way, also he sells it, you know?"

"Sells it, sells it to who?"

"Well, keep it quiet, but he sells some to the golf and rugby clubs."

"Cool, your dad's a bootlegger."

"Yeah, something like that."

We reach the bottom of the hill that leads to Tawton Heights. The hill in front of us is very steep with various-sized detached houses on either side of it.

"Right, just think all, at the top of this hill there are treats, lots of treats. Come on, Robbie, I bet I get to mine before you can."

Boys, boys, always making a game out of something. Me and Tanya slowly make our way up the incline, we don't talk, we just lean slightly forward and walk. I notice the orange streetlights slowly flicker and come on, I glance at my phone and see that it is a quarter to eight.

About halfway up the hill me and Tanya stop for a breather.

"Jesus, this bloody hill, my legs are aching, Fran, are yours?"

"I am out of breath; I am never smoking again! My legs are okay, it's my chest, it feels really tight."

"I know, we can swim like fish, but this really takes it out of me."

"True. I am feeling better though, Tan, I think I just got a bit spun out by all the people and the noise. Let's have some more of that powder, and drink some more, I really am having a good time.

"Do you think Robbie likes me? I mean he's quite good-looking, isn't he?"

"Ooh, you like him, you love him; of course, he likes you, Teddy says he talks about you a lot."

"Really, what does he say?"

"Just that he thinks you're good-looking, and he thinks you are fit."

"Never! That's good."

"Well, let's get up to Teddy's, and you can get to know him a bit better."

We carry on up the hill, nearing the driveway that leads through the front garden towards the front of Teddy's house. In the driveway I notice Teddy's mum's white BMW, it's always so clean; when I see it speeding through the town it's unmistakable because of its bright, sparkling white cleanliness.

We reach the already open front door and Teddy waves us in. Once inside, the house looks a lot like the picture I had imagined in my mind. Big, spotlessly clean, nicely furnished rooms, with lots of mirrors and ornaments on the shelves, with thick rugs on the floors, and a sweet candle smell throughout.

"Tan, Fran, come through to the kitchen."

The kitchen is all white and tiled, there is a large stainless-steel cooker, a long, dark wooden table, and I spot one of those American fridges with an ice maker.

"Have a seat, can I get you anything, a Coke or 7up?"

"I'll have a Coke, please; can I use your ice maker?"

"Sure, I'll get you a glass. Tan, Robbie, want anything?"

"The same, please."

"Yeah, and me."

The cold Coke fizz refreshes my mouth, it tastes so good with ice. I drink it down fast and give out a satisfying sigh. Robbie comes and sits opposite me; I notice Teddy and Tanya having a passionate hug and kiss by the fridge.

"You enjoying that legal high stuff? I love it, Teddy and me get it from a bloke in Okement."

"Yeah, it's nice, I didn't know what it would do, but I feel so full of energy, I haven't stopped talking really."

"I know, I did notice, it's a stimulant so it does that, it's like drinking twenty cups of strong coffee or something."

"Yeah, it's definitely a stimulant then, I love coffee, my favourite is a flat white, I get one from Fat Eddie's now and again, it always seems to wake me up."

"My favourite is a cappuccino; I love the froth."

"Right, you two, sorry to interrupt the love-in, but I am not sure what time my parents are coming back. So, let's do a quick line here, and then I'll grab another bottle. Robbie grab a couple of Cokes from the fridge."

We take in turns to do a line; these lines are much longer and thicker than before. Teddy chopped up the powder on his Mum's black granite chopping board, and I guess it was easier then messing around on the back of a plastic phone.

"Wow! That was the one, that's going to hit the spot."

"Nice one, Teddy, that was a proper line. I've got the Cokes; shall we exit?"

We do just that, exiting through Teddy's front door. As I walk, I take that now familiar hard swallow, and clear my nose. That line quickly sends a stronger tingle to my head, and then to my toes; it all feels nice and warm again.

"Come on, come on, let's run down the hill."

We all follow Teddy's lead.

"Whoa, that's fast, hold my arm, Robbie, I am going to fall."

"I've got you, don't make me fall, keep hold of my hand."

"Teddy, slow down, wait for me, love."

We all come to rest against a wooden fence that sits at the bottom of the hill, outside one of the houses. We are all out of breath but start laughing, laughing together out loud.

"Yes! That's getting the chemicals working, whoa, I thought you were going to fall then, Fran."

"And me, but thanks to you I made it."

"Anytime."

The laughing, the non-stop talking continues as we head back towards the river. The daylight is fading quickly, and by the time we get back to the sports fields the night has drawn in. We stop for a rest on an old, wooden park bench, which sits facing the now empty football pitch. Teddy offers his fags around; we share his lighter and sit back onto the bench.

"God, this stuff makes you want to smoke, doesn't it? I've never smoked so much; it's not going to help my lungs for swimming."

"Good, maybe next swim I can catch-up with you, keep smoking, Fran."

"Nasty, no it was a good race, just my day, that's all."

"I bet you both look fit in your swimsuits."

"Oh, perv."

"What? It's a compliment, I would like to see Fran in hers."

"I've seen Tan in hers, gorgeous!"

"Shush, Teddy, that's our secret."

"Robbie, if you are lucky, you might see me in mine."

"Lucky is my middle name, Fran."

We all chuckle; Tanya is a flirt, but that was something new from me. I guess boys would find me a bit attractive, but with me always being around Tanya, the boy's attention surely would be more on her, and her bronzed skin, athletic body, big blue eyes and long, curly, blonde hair.

The attention from Robbie makes me feel good, I haven't had that before. I am enjoying being around him.

We finish our fags and make our way towards the river. Tanya and Teddy walk on ahead, and

Robbie and I walk together, side by side, just talking, joking, and laughing together.

***

"Fran, calm down, just calm down, breathe, take some deep breaths. Teddy, help! Fran's spinning out big time."

"What can I do?"

"I don't know, just try and calm her down."

"Fran! Listen, listen you'll be fine, you're just having a moment, you've just taken too much, it's your first time. I've spun out before, but it goes away, honestly it does go away."

"No, no it's not stopping, my heart, make it stop!"

"Keep taking deep breaths, your heart is racing because of the drugs, it will pass."

"I can't, I can't do it, I want to go home… Mum, I want to go home, what have I done."

"Your mum's coming home next week, Fran, that will be good, won't it? I mean, that's good news, isn't it?"

"No, no, I can't see Mum like this, can't go home like this, how long is it going to last, Tan?"

"You don't have to go home, Fran, you're staying at mine remember? Just breathe, it won't last for much longer, I promise."

"No, I need to get home, see Pip, Pip doesn't understand, she needs me, just make it stop."

"Fran, mate, you're not making any sense, come on, let's go back to mine, you can go straight to bed if you want."

"I can't move, Tan, I won't move, I can't see straight, my heart is going to stop! It's going to burst."

"Mate, it's not, it's just the effects from the drug, this has happened to Teddy before. Right, Teddy?"

"Yeah, honestly, Fran, I know it's not nice, but it has happened to me, it happened to Robbie too. We thought our heart was never going to slow down, but it did. You just need to go to Tanya's and sleep it off."

"Can't go, I can't move, just let me sleep here, I can't sleep, just leave me here."

"Were not leaving you, mate, you can't stay here, Fran, it's getting cold, and my mum's going to start wondering where we are. I told her we would be home by ten."

"Get my dad, I want my dad now! I can't feel like this, am I dying? I think I'm dying."

"Fran, you're not dying mate, we can't call your dad, your dad will go mad, just think; come back to mine, and I'll look after you, we can share my bed if you want, we could just get under the covers and chill out."

"Leave me alone, you don't understand; Tanya just go, go away with Teddy, I'll be okay, just leave me here, in half an hour or so I'll be fine."

"Can't do that, Fran, won't do that, you need to come home with me, come on, mate, please, let's go."

"Leave, just leave me here to die."

"Tan, what are we going to do? Me and Robbie have got to get going. Robbie's staying at mine, and my mum's expecting us back by ten at the latest."

"Ah, God, I don't know, what time is it now?"

"Nine thirty. I don't want to leave you in the shit, but if we are not back by ten then my dad will freak."

"You can't leave me! Teddy you can't leave me here, what am I supposed to do?"

"Fran, Fran, look at me, it's Teddy; you've got to get going, come on go home with Tanya, we could carry you for a bit if you want? But you are not staying here, we can't leave you here, it's getting cold. We don't want to call your dad either, he's going to freak out. Just go back to Tan's, you'll feel better in the morning, I promise, just have a sleep, Tan will look after you."

"No! I said no. I'm not going home... take me home, Pip and Tom need me home."

"Right! Ted, this is getting bloody stupid, she's not making any sense, let's grab an arm each and get her back to Tan's, I can't listen to this anymore, you shouldn't have given her any more of that, I could see she was getting wasted, I told you no more. We've had two bottles of vodka, and two grams of that. It's time to go, if we don't sort this right now, I am going back to mine, this is bad, mate."

"Thanks, Robbie, big help, you were the one who wanted to sniff some more, you were the one who wanted to get to know Franny better, remember? 'Oh, she's lovely, get us together, Teddy, she's so fit, does she like me?' Fine, bloody brilliant, grab an arm then, I've had enough of this."

"Get off me, don't touch me; Tanya, get them off me, I'm calling my dad."

"Fran, for Christ sake! We are trying to help you. If we call your dad, what's going to happen? I tell you what's going to happen, he's going to get mad, he's going to want to know why you are in this state, he won't be happy until he's found out what's gone on tonight. He'll confront our parents, ask where the drugs have come from, how we got the booze, it's going to be a bloody nightmare, mate."

"I don't care, I don't care! I want my dad, I want this to stop, I want my dad now!"

"Okay, okay, Fran. Is that what you really want? Fuck it, call her dad; just tell him Fran's drunk too much, just tell him sorry but Fran's just over done it with the booze, he can't think that his

138

daughter hasn't ever had a drink before; tell him we are near the park, you know by the park bench where we all sat earlier. I don't care anymore, me and Robbie will carry her kicking and screaming if need be, we've got to get going."

"Fran, did you hear that? Is that what you really want? I'll call your dad, use your phone, but he's not going to be happy, is he? Just tell him you've had some vodka, just tell him you haven't eaten anything and feel a bit sick, okay? Blame me if you want, just say I got a little bottle of vodka and didn't realise how strong it was, just say something like that."

"I will, I will say that I've got to go home, sorry, Tan, sorry everyone. I can't do this, I feel awful, I feel outside my body, you won't understand, I can't stay here, I need to go home."

"Call then, call Frankie, call Fran's dad, Tan. We could get her to that bench in five minutes, ring Frankie now and by the time he gets there, me and Robbie would have left."

"You're not going to wait with me, Teddy?"

"Sorry, babe, no chance, we'll have to head off."

"Thanks, that's a chicken shit move."

"Please, I've supplied all the booze, all the drugs, what have you done apart from bring along this lightweight?"

"Nice; lovely attitude, just go then. I'll get her to the bench; I wouldn't want you to put yourself out. God, I won't forget this, Teddy."

"I didn't mean it like that, you know I didn't mean it like that. I can't stay around if Fran's dad is turning up, I can't be there for that, he'll crucify us."

"Fine, it's down to me then, down to me, just for a change. Just go then, go!"

"Oh, fuck this, fine, we are going, come on Robbie... Robbie! Come on."

"I don't know, Teddy, it doesn't seem right."

"Forget right or wrong, do you want to be around when Frankie Doors turns up and wants to know what's happened to his daughter? No way, we've got to go."

"Sorry, Tan, I've got to go with Teddy, sorry."

"Fine... gutless, both of you. I'll remind you of this, I'll remind you every bloody day."

"Fran, Fran, give me your phone, love. I am going to call your dad, let's get you home, ah? I'll ring him, but let's meet him at that park bench, not down here, not down here with the empty bottles and fag ends."

"Thanks, Tan, I am never doing this again, never again."

"I know, I know, just give me your phone, Fran."

"Hi. Is that Frankie? Hi, it's Tanya... Tanya, Franny's best friend from school."

"What's happened? What's happened, Tanya? I can't hear you clearly, what's happened?"

"Nothing serious, honestly, it's my fault, I got us a little bottle of vodka, and I think Fran's drunk too much, so sorry, Frankie, she's asking for you, I think she just wants to go home."

"Oh shit, has she been sick?"

"No, not sick but I think she just wants to get home and go to bed, sorry, Frankie."

"Okay, where is she? At yours? Shall I walk up and get her?"

"We were, now we're down at the park."

"The park! I thought you were having a girly night in at yours?"

"That was the plan, it's my fault, Frankie, I nicked a small bottle of vodka from my mum's stash, I didn't think it was going to end up like this."

"All right, all right, no big deal, where exactly are you then?"

"The park, the old park bench that is opposite the football pitch."

"Okay, give me ten minutes, I'll be there, just wait for me there."

"Will do, see you soon, sorry."

"Fran, your dad's on his way. That's what you wanted, yes? Remember, it's just that you have drunk too much, that's all. I've told him that we have had some vodka, and it's my fault. Just get back home, drink some water and go to bed and I'll ring you first thing tomorrow.

"Come on then, babe, let's have a walk. Your dad's going to meet us at that park bench, he's only ten minutes away."

"I am so sorry, Tan. Have Teddy and Robbie gone?"

"Yeah, they both disappeared like rats down a drainpipe. Rats, that's a good word for them both, gutless rats. Come on, mate, let's get to that bench, your dad will be there soon."

"He's going to hate me, Tan, my dad's going to hate me."

"No, he won't. I've told him it's my fault, I told him we drunk some vodka, that's it, don't mention the drugs, Fran, there's no need to mention the drugs."

"He's not stupid, Tan, my dad's going to know its more than just some vodka."

"I don't know what to say, Fran, you've got to convince him it's just that you've drunk too much."

"I'll try, how long does this drug last though? I mean everything's going at a hundred miles per hour."

"Oh, mate, it lasts a while, we've taken a lot, come on get up."

I slowly get myself up from the stony riverbed, my whole body feels sick, my legs are numb, and my arms are tingling, like pins and needles. Tanya takes my arm, and I lean on her like I've never lent on anybody before. I need her support just to stand up straight. The drink, the drugs have messed me up, I feel my chest, my heart is pumping, my head is full of scattered thoughts; my dad, my mum, what are they going to think? Aunty Pam, God seeing Aunty Pam in this state. Am I ever going to feel normal again, I wish I could go back to earlier, I would have decided to stay at home.

Just an hour or so ago I was full of it, full of life, my head full of all possibilities, loving the moment. But now I feel sick, sick to the stomach, my body doesn't seem to belong to me, it's like I am looking at myself, watching myself from some far-off place.

"I've got you, Fran, nearly there. God, we won't forget this in a hurry, will we? Oh, don't cry, Fran, you'll get me started. It's going to be okay; we won't ever do this again; I am so sorry."

"It's not your fault, I've felt weird, strange all day, since seeing my mum. Even before seeing her, I've felt panicky, yeah that's the word, panicky, I've felt panicky for a while now."

"Well, I am not surprised that you've been feeling like that. I mean you have so much to deal with, you're like a mum to Tom and Pip, it's a lot to cope with, Fran."

"I know, but what else am I supposed to do."

"Yeah, I know, it's hard on you though, it must be so hard. I am here for you though, I'll always be here for you, Fran."

"Oh, thanks, and me."

"Look, we are nearly at the bench, your dad won't be long now."

***

"Girls, you okay? What the hell is going on? I was enjoying my pint with the lads."

"Oh, Dad, Dad I feel awful, sorry it's all my fault, I drank too much vodka."

"No, it's my fault, Frankie, I didn't realise it was so strong."

"Okay, okay, let's not worry about whose fault it is, let's have a look at you, love, come on, my love, let's have a look at you."

"I can't, Dad, I feel so ashamed, I've ruined everything, haven't I?

"Ruined! Don't be so dramatic, love, give your dad a hug. Honestly, I'm just happy you both felt you could call me; thanks for that, Tanya, by the way. Seriously, I would rather you both feel that you could call me and let me know that you need my help than think that you couldn't. So, come on,

Fran, it'll be okay, give me a hug, love, tell me what's wrong."

I fall forward almost over dramatically into my dad's arms; I suddenly feel all off balance and my head is in a real mess.

Having Dad here, and him wanting to hold me tight and tell me everything's going to be all right feels good; it makes me feel happy and sad, all at the same time.

"Right, let's get you home. Tanya can we walk you back home first?"

"Thanks, but no, it's not far and I am sure Fran just wants to get to bed."

"Well, if you are sure? It's not a problem."

"Honestly, thanks, but I'll be fine. Fran, just get some sleep, mate, so sorry for all of this."

"Just get home safe, you. Thanks again for calling, Tanya. Fran, say goodbye to Tanya."

"Thanks, Tan, I'll speak tomorrow, loves you."

"And you, speak tomorrow."

"Right, take my arm, love, and let's get you home, you can tell me what you have taken in the morning."

"Ah… Dad, it's just been the vodka."

"I am not stupid, love, you and Tanya's eyes are massive, and she couldn't stop fidgeting around, so you will tell me in the morning, okay? When we get home, I want you to go straight upstairs to bed, I'll bring you up a glass of water, and you must just try to sleep. Okay? Okay, love?"

"Yes."

I do just that, I can't really recall the walk home after Dad had said those words. I've pissed him off big time, I've lied to him, and he knows it. I should have known not to think I could fob him off with only half a story.

Once inside the front door I quickly head upstairs, I don't even look into the front room, I just race up to my bedroom. In my room, I just sit at first, just sit on the edge of my bed. *Am I ever going to feel like myself again, what have I done? I feel horrible, my head is spinning.*

***

"Frankie, didn't expect you back so early, what's happened? Why's Fran home?"

"She's had a drink, by the look of it, she's had a big drink. Tanya called me when I was at the club. She was in a panic; they were down at the park and Fran had drunk some vodka or something and was asking for me."

"Well, I knew she was with Tanya, but I thought Fran was staying in, and having a girly night, DVDs and all that."

"Me too, but hey, they are teenagers. Tanya got hold of some vodka, they must have decided to drink it in the park. They wouldn't be the first, would they?"

"Well, maybe not, has she been sick?"

"Not yet, I wouldn't be surprised if she is though, I am going to take some water up."

"Take the kitchen bowl as well then, just in case."

"Will do, good thinking. How have Tom and Pip been?"

"Great, Tom came home about six o'clock, he and Noah played some Xbox for a while, then I made them some tuna and pasta. They loved that, and then Noah left just before seven. Pip watched the boys play, and then I put on her *Sponge Bob Square Pants*. She never gets fed up with that, does she?"

"Never, I think I've seen it over a hundred times, she loves it."

"Have you eaten?"

"I had a little bowl of pasta, but that's it."

"Do you fancy a takeaway, my treat?"

"Could do. What you thinking? Chinese?"

"Oh, yeah. Chinese would be good right now; I'll get the menu."

"Shall we get something for Franny?"

"No, Pam, I don't think she could stomach anything at the moment."

"Right, yeah, I just worry that she hasn't had any tea."

"Fran will be fine, Pam, food is not going to help her, she probably hasn't got an appetite anyway."

***

I haven't undressed, my duvet is covering me all the way up to my chin. I've tried to shut my eyes, but quickly realised that was a no go. As soon as I did, the room, then my bed felt like it was spinning around. I've managed to kick off my trainers, but then I felt a chill all over me, like having the flu or something. I start shaking, and my teeth start chattering. I quickly get under my duvet and it takes an age before I begin to feel any warmth. I can hear the muffled talking from downstairs and picture Dad and Pam talking about me.

My room is in darkness apart from the orange glow of the streetlights that streams a little light through my cloth curtains. I concentrate my eyes towards my chest, the duvet is moving repeatedly, quickly up and down like a machine. I can only interrupt the pumping rhythm by taking a deep forced breath. The machine-like motion then returns, and it feels like the only thing in my whole wide world. How long have I been lying here? It feels like an age. I resist the need for going for a pee, I don't want that chill again. I can't move anyway. I move my focus away from my chest and try to move my toes, they feel cold, really cold. I do manage to move them; they crack like a twig and might break.

God, I need to pee; I dismiss it again but then can only think about doing it. I don't want to move; I really don't know if I can move. Just moving my head to look again at my rising duvet is hard enough. I can't find any comfort, I would normally hug my pillows, wrap the duvet around my legs, like a snake would constrict its prey.

"Fran, can I come in? I've got your water, love."

Shit, I forgotten about that, surely it's been ages since I got in.

"Fran, I'm coming in, I've got your water."

Dad enters my bedroom, and his big frame fills the doorway, like a giant silhouette. I look again and now only see the glare of the landing light behind him.

"Just try and drink some, love. How you feeling?"

I force a smile, but doubt Dad would have noticed that in the dark.

"Yeah, okay, Dad. I just want to sleep."

"Okay, I'll leave you to it. I am not angry, love; disappointed, but not angry. Just try and get some sleep and we'll talk more tomorrow."

"Thanks, Dad."

Dad shuts my door and from somewhere deep inside I suddenly feel full of guilt and fear; I begin to cry uncontrollably. What have I done? I just want to curl up and disappear. Surely the drugs must be leaving my body by now. I feel thirsty, water would be good, my mouth is so dry, but I daren't move. My arms are finally starting to feel warm, so I don't reach out for the pint glass which is just sitting inches away on my bedside table.

I spend what seems like hours just staring vaguely around my room, but my eyes keep returning to my chest and its fast, repetitive beat, rising and falling under my duvet. I want to just switch it off, but I can't, my mind is racing, and my thoughts are only able to focus on the bleak and the dark. Is this what dying feels like?

My message tone sounds, and it makes my skin jump, my heart feels like it's just missed a beat. It's got to be Tanya, but no way am I answering that. I don't even know where my phone is, maybe on my bedroom floor, but it's definitely not on me.

I finally manage to close my eyes without the room seeming to spin. I move my toes again, but my feet even in my socks feel icy cold. With my eyes closed all my senses seem to heighten, pins and needles surge all over my body, my head is foggy, and the only smell I can smell is that of stale tobacco in the air. Everything is wrong, when will I feel normal again? I focus on keeping my eyes shut, my eyelids flutter as to remind me that I am not tired. I am tired though, tired of feeling that something awful is just about to happen.

Knock, knock. I am startled by the sound, it's the front door. Who could it be? Was I asleep? What time is it? My eyes are wide open once again. The sound of the front door; has it woken me or am I dreaming it?

For one moment I imagine it's the police, they've come to arrest me for taking drugs and underage drinking. Panicking, I pull the duvet up over my face. I can just make out my dad's voice and one other, which I don't recognise. The conversation seems short, and then in what seems like seconds I hear the front door shutting.

I keep my duvet resting over my face, I take some comfort in feeling my hot breath on that soft, warm material.

Shutting my eyes again, I drift from wildly imagining who was at the front door, to does it really matter?

I feel myself drift now, in and out of a disturbing kind of sleep. Every time I think my heart is slowing, that single thought is enough to send my heart racing all over again. When I open my eyes my room seems different, the long mirror which stands in the far corner of my bedroom is reflecting strange, scary shapes onto my white walls. The twisted forms of these shapes take on an animal type figure, like a dragon, I flicker my eye lids hoping to clear those images from my sight, but it doesn't work, the images become scarier as I notice a large wide-open, sharpened tooth filled mouth.

God, what is going on? I feel so scared, scared of the shadows that linger in the corners of my room, my pile of clean clothes, which are on my chair, takes on an angry dog form. I can make out a large square head and long pointy nose. Again, I pull my duvet over my head. This time I wrap the top of it tightly around my head. There is no way I'm moving from this position, I can't see in the black darkness beneath the duvet, that's fine because I'm too scared to look anymore, just please let me sleep.

Being cocooned like this only makes me more aware of my quick, panicky breaths, the lack of fresh air and the close hot bedding surrounding me only heightens my hearing. I can hear the machine-like thud of my rapid heartbeat. Again, sweat begins to form, but this time it's all over my body, I feel hot, flushed and can smell my breath under the duvet.

I fearfully stick my head out from under my covers, I don't open my eyes, I just take a big breath out and then inhale some colder air in. Once again I tightly wrap my duvet around and over my head.

After what feels like hours, I find myself hiding under the covers in exactly the same position as before. I come around slowly from a scary dream about being bitten by large fang-toothed dog. The dog wouldn't stop grabbing at my hand, I tried to fight it off, but it just kept coming back, taking larger bites at my flesh.

Becoming more awake now, I start to hear the familiar sounds of the bird's morning song; Christ, it can't be morning already, can it? I haven't really slept at all I don't think.

Their morning song sounds louder than normal, their now high-pitched sounding shrills seem to penetrate through the walls of my room and straight into my head. The noise triggers in me a memory, a memory of flashing blue lights and wailing sirens, a picture of my mum flashes again in my mind. Her grey, sunken, lifeless, distorted face, and her pale, skinny, limp white arms and legs.

Chapter 4

"Morning, Dad."

"Morning, my boy. How did you sleep?"

"Really good. I heard you come home though, then someone came running up the stairs."

"Yeah, that was your sister, she had a bad night."

"Ah, what, fell out with Tanya, did she?"

"No, nothing like that, love. Fran decided to drink some vodka with Tanya, then she was feeling ill."

"Ah, okay."

"Anyway, enough of that for now, what you having for brekkie? I was going to cook some bacon; you fancy one of your dad's famous doorstep sarnies?"

"Cool, yeah, thanks, Dad. Is Pip still asleep?"

"She is, love, I'll pop up, and check on her in a minute."

***

What usually wakes us? Could it be the daylight streaming through your window? Or maybe you've set an alarm for work or school? It might just be the noise of the morning bin men?

This morning I awake to the smell of frying bacon and strong, brewing coffee; those first few seconds of waking are disorientating at best. This morning my eyelids are refusing to fully open. I take a deep breath in through my nose and that salty frying smell, so recognisable, usually so welcome, turns my sickly stomach over and over again.

I bury my head deep into my pillows, and then quickly pull up my duvet over my head. The memories, the distorted thoughts, flashes of moments from yesterday, begin their attack. Attack is the right word, countless thoughts come rushing in from every angle: my mum, Tanya, vodka, snorting that bloody stuff, Robbie, Teddy's house, the park, the river, my dad and that awful all-over feeling of being scared; scared of every sound or thought.

As soon as those thoughts have entered my mind, I become aware of how my body feels. I guess however you normally wake up, you just naturally become aware of your thoughts, you then become aware of how your body feels. Say your limbs are aching from swimming, or you have slept awkwardly on your arm, or on your neck. This morning I become aware that my body from head to toe feels so different, different from any other feeling that I have ever felt before.

My thoughts are interrupted by footsteps coming up the stairs. *Please don't come in, I can't face anyone*, I think to myself.

The footsteps sound heavy and purposeful, it must be my dad. I breathe a huge sigh of relief when I hear Pip's squeaky bedroom door being opened.

I hear Dad's distinctive deep voice.

"Ah, you're awake, my little Pip, good morning, gorgeous."

"Da, Dad, *SpongeBob* on."

"Yeah, yeah, we will, love, come on then, arms up, let's have some brekkie, shall we?"

I follow the footsteps as Dad and Pip head down the stairs. I really don't want to move but the need for the toilet, which I've been putting off for most of the night, is now becoming beyond my control. The dull discomfort of earlier has now become a constant pain. I slowly get out of my bed and feel faint as soon as I am on my feet. I just stand there, willing myself to move, everything is wrong. I finally open my door and quietly tiptoe across the landing; I don't want to be seen; I don't want to be heard. *Just use the toilet and get straight back into bed.*

I consider not flushing the toilet, the sound would surely draw attention to me being awake. *God, why am I thinking like this*? I push the flush and tip toe back to my room, I quickly get under my duvet, feeling scared of every movement, sound, or thought.

***

"Tom, get the little plates out, oh, and the brown and red sauce please."

"Okay, Dad, will do."

"Pip, you want a bowl of Sugar Puffs? Or maybe try a little bacon sarnie for a change?"

"Um, sugar huffs please, Dad."

"Okay, coming up, my little one."

***

Lying flat on my back, I feel a chill all over my body. I sit up and reach for my glass of water, gulping down half a pint of the now warming liquid. I drink it so fast that I spill most of it all over my chin. As I settle back down under my duvet, my phone rings, it startles me at first. I look on the floor next to my bed but can't see it. The ringtone continues and finally I find it on the floor at the foot of my bed.

I can see I've had two new messages and one missed call, all from Tanya. I think about replying, but just the thought of finding the right words makes my head hurt. Instead I just lay back, shut my eyes and try to relax.

***

"Oh, Tom answer my phone, love, I've got my hands full here in the kitchen."

"It's Pam, hi, Aunty Pam. Dad's coming, he's just cooking some bacon."

"Okay, love, shall I call back?"

"Dad, do you want Aunty Pam to call you back?"

"Could do… no, say I will call, I'll call her in twenty minutes or so."

"Aunty Pam, Dad's going to call you back in twenty."

"Okay, love, no problem."

"God, she's ringing early. Right, sarnies are on their way, grab a seat Tom, Pip, come on, love, breakfast."

"Look at the size of that! Dad, that's massive."

"A Dad special coming up, my love, doorstep bread with real butter and four rashers of bacon, that'll put hairs on your chest, my boy!"

"Cool, have you made one for Fran?"

"No, I think food is a little way off for your sister, love, I'll check on her after brekkie. We could have a walk to the park later if you want? Pam is heading over to see your mum a bit later, I guess she was calling to see if Fran is okay."

"The park sounds good. Is Fran in big trouble, Dad?"

"Not big, just a little bit. I think Fran may have learnt a valuable lesson last night, I am just pleased Tanya rang and I got her home safe. How's your sarnie?"

"Delicious, I can't fit it in my mouth, Dad!"

"Ha-ha, get it down you, boy; Pip, little orange Pip, you want some more cereal?"

"Um, no thanks da, da, full."

"Full, full big belly, love, have you?"

"Belly big."

***

I can't stay in bed all day; no way is Dad going to let me do that. The thought of getting up, changing my clothes, facing Dad, seeing Tom and Pip, fills me with dread. I've been ill before, of course, but this, this sickness is in my head, isn't it? My thoughts turn to the day ahead. Dad's going to want to know what happened last night, he's going to shout, what can I say? Dad's not stupid, he'll push me about everything. God, school, I can't go to school feeling like this.

Every thought I have seems to produce a physical reaction, my heart goes faster, my legs and stomach-ache, I feel so ill. *Just stop, please stop.* Frustrated, confused, I hide under my duvet again.

***

"Finished, love?"

"Yeah, I can't eat the crusts though, Dad, I am stuffed."

"You did well, my boy, go and watch TV with Pip, love; I'll call Pam and then clean up."

"Thanks, Dad. Come on, Pip, let's watch *SpongeBob*."

"Yeah, *SpongeBob*, *SpongeBob Adventures*."

"Tom, turn the volume down a little, I'm giving Pam a call."

"Hi, Pam, you okay?"

"Yeah, just checking in on Fran, how is she?"

"Not sure to be honest, she's still in bed. You seeing Launa this morning?"

"Yes, planning to get over there for eleven. I thought I would take her for a walk, maybe down to Frew's Slope, have a picnic or something."

"Lovely, weather looks good, Launa will love that. Fran's going to be okay, Pam. I'll leave her sleeping for a bit, then have a chat with her later."

"Okay, Frankie, I won't say anything to Launa, I'll give you a call later and let you know how the day has gone, okay?"

"Great, thanks, Pam, give her a kiss from me, oh, and tell her I'll call tomorrow as normal."

"Will do, speak later."

"You both okay in there? Tom, keep an eye on your sister, I am going to clean up, then have a chat with Fran."

"Okay, we are fine, Dad."

***

I try and make myself sick by sticking two fingers down my throat, just get it out of me, just get this feeling out of me. I retch and only bring up a little frothy yellow phlegm; it sticks to my fingers like stringy glue and feeling like I do I just wipe it onto my duvet. Feeling worse after that, I take a sip of water, my mouth tastes awful, there is a bitter, dry film all over my teeth.

"Can I come in, love?"

"Oh, Dad, I am being sick."

"Use the bowl, I put it by your bed last night, can I come in?"

"No, I just need to sleep, Dad, I need to sleep."

"I am coming in, love."

My dad's face looks distorted to me, he's wearing his black tracksuit and it looks too tight on him, I notice he has bare feet, and his top is splattered with what looks like water splashes.

"Oh, love, look at you, have you been sick?"

"A little bit, I don't feel right, Dad."

"Well you won't, will you? Come on, love, try and sit up."

"I can't, Dad, can I just sleep some more, please? I'll be okay, I just need to sleep."

"You have slept, love, it's nearly ten o'clock, we've been up since nine. I've cooked bacon, Aunty Pam has rung, and Tom and Pip are now watching *SpongeBob*. So, it's time we talked."

"Can we talk later? Please, Dad, please."

"Well, when then? I was planning on taking Pip and Tom down to the park, you need to tell me what went on last night. I know it wasn't just vodka, Fran. I am worried, worried about you."

"Oh, don't, Dad. I will tell you everything, but I am so ill right now, can we just speak later, please?"

"No, sorry, Fran, I need to know what you've taken. I am not going to leave you here. I mean what if something happens to you when I am out?"

"Nothing's going to happen to me, Dad, I just need to rest, then I can talk about it later."

"No, love, I'll get you some more water and then we can talk; it won't take long, and then you can rest."

It won't take long. Oh, I think it's going to take a while, I am not sure how to voice how I feel. It would be easier for me if Dad would just let me rest for a while, but that's not going to happen. Dad wants answers, and it seems there is no way out of that. As Dad heads to the bathroom, I try to run through in my mind what I could say, then instantly doubt that my version, my lies, would satisfy him.

"Right, try and drink some water, love; you must be dehydrated."

"I am thirsty, I have been sick a few times, Dad."

"Oh, Fran. Do you still feel sick now?"

"Yeah, I do. So sorry, I feel awful."

"Well, you were obviously drunk, but come on, Fran, your dad's been around a bit, what else did you have?"

"Nothing, I... just drunk too much vodka, it was so strong."

"Fran, love, I am not going to shout, but we need to talk about it, honestly, I just want to make sure you're okay."

"I had some cigarettes, and lots of vodka, that's it."

"What you smoking for? God, Fran, that's going to stop your swimming, you'll never make a go of it if you smoke."

"I know, I won't do it again."

"Well, I hope so. It's hard, love; I smoke, I know it's not good, but I don't want you to follow in my footsteps. I've made plenty of mistakes, I have lots of regrets, but, Fran, you could really make something of your life."

"I won't smoke again, Dad, I only did it because everyone else was."

"Everyone, who else was there then."

"Just Teddy, you know, Tanya's boyfriend."

"He had the drugs then, did he?"

"No! Dad, I can't do this now, I feel so unwell. Can I please just sleep some more?"

"Sorry, no. I am not going until you tell me what you've taken. You said you were spending a girly night in with Tanya. You ended up in the park, and now you tell me Teddy was there. Who else was there?"

"No one, Dad, please, I think I am going to be sick again."

"I'll just wash the bowl out, just give me a minute."

I feel sick, but don't need to be physically sick. Dad's pushing me, and I can't face it. I see the strain on his face and don't want to stress him out even more. Again, I stick my fingers back down my throat, I retch hard, and then uncontrollably start to choke. Nothing really comes up though, all I can taste, and feel is a bitter, frothy chemical phlegm in my mouth.

"Here's the bowl, do you need it?"

"Not right now, no."

"Right, it's on the floor if you need it. The sooner you tell me what went on last night, the quicker you can sleep some more."

"Oh, Dad, it was just me Teddy and Tanya; we all drunk some vodka. Teddy had the bottle and we mixed it with some Coke."

"Yeah, I guessed that much, love, but what else did you all take?"

"Nothing, I drunk so much, that's why I feel so horrible, I won't do it again, I promise."

"Promises aren't going to do it, love. I knew, just looking at you last night, that you had taken something, Tanya was all over the place, too. So, what was it? Speed, cocaine, it wasn't weed, was it? I could tell you were racing; Tanya was talking at a hundred miles an hour; your eyes were dilated, and you were both sweating buckets."

"Okay… okay, Dad, I did try something, it was one of those legal highs. I am so sorry, I feel awful, I won't ever do it again."

"I bloody hope so, honestly, Fran. I know things are tough, I know it's a shit time right now, but these so-called legal highs are dangerous, you know. There was that thing on the news, just a few days ago, remember? A boy from up north, he took some legal high drug and died."

"I know, Dad, I can't explain why, but I just did it."

"What was it, what is it called?"

"Benzo, something, Benzo Fury, I think, it's a powder. Tanya said it's like drinking lots of strong coffee."

"Stupid, bloody crazy, that's the one that killed that boy, something to do with his heart. Honestly, love, don't you go near that stuff again, these drugs will mess your head up, I've got enough on my plate without all this. I suggest you take a shower, get some clean clothes on and try to eat something. I promised the kids a walk to the park this morning, so get yourself sorted and I'll see you when we get back."

"I will, sorry, I don't feel right though, Dad."

"Well, you're not going to feel great, are you? With all that stuff in your system, mixed with God knows how much vodka. Have a shower, Fran. Have some toast, your stomach needs some food."

Dad leaves my room, and for a split second I feel relieved; he had to know, there was no way out of it. What I couldn't really tell him was how I feel. I don't understand how I feel, talking to Dad was difficult, his face looked twisted. Now the whole room is distorted somehow, the posters on my wall seem to be moving, the colours mixing and flowing into each other. I shake my head, and glance away from those troubling images.

The thought of having a shower, cleaning my teeth, somehow seems pointless. I do change, but just slip on my tracksuit and change my socks. Back in bed again, I try to rest, my thoughts are everywhere, I'm unable to concentrate on anything.

***

"Wakey, wakey its two o'clock. Fran, come on, love, I've made you a sandwich, your favourite tuna salad with cheese."

"Ah, okay, come in."

"How you doing? Have you had a shower? I popped in on you an hour or so ago, but you were fast asleep, you feeling any better?"

"I don't know yet, I guess some sleep has helped."

"Good, try and eat something then; I think it's time you got up, love. Oh, don't cry, love, you'll be okay, just get that shit out of your body, and you'll be fine."

"I can't, Dad, I don't know what's happening to me. I can't see straight, everything's wrong, my heart won't stop racing, my whole body feels weird, I think I need a doctor."

"Oh, love, you may think you need a doctor, but it's just a very bad hangover with the side-effects of that drug on top. Listen, when you take any type of drug there is what's called a come-down. That means your body is feeling the aftereffects of what you have taken, it's horrible, I know, but it does pass."

"It's not passing, it's getting worse, I think it's a virus or something, I can't breathe properly."

"Just try some deep breaths, love. Honestly, Fran, the feelings you're having are just the effects of what you've put in your body. Calm down, love, breathe. What can I do?"

"Dad, I think I am going to faint, Dad!"

"Deep breaths, come on just take some deep breaths, in and out, that's it, in through your nose, out through your mouth."

I think I am dying; my breaths are rapid. Dad puts his arm around me and tells me to focus on my breathing. I try, but still l can't slow my heart rate down. A horrible tingle, like pins and needles soar all over and through my body, sweat returns onto my forehead and I smell a sweet sickly smell all around me.

"Come on, Fran, concentrate, you're getting yourself in hell of a state here. It will pass. Try counting to ten, then breathe out."

I can't stop crying, my tears sting my tired eyes, so I bury my head into my pillows wiping my eyes and nose as I do so. One, two, three, I count to myself, trying to concentrate like Dad said.

"That's it, my love, that's better, your breathing is slowing down."

"Oh, God, what's happening, Dad? This can't just be the drugs, can it?"

"I think so, I don't know enough about what you've taken, but if it's a stimulant, like coffee – didn't Tanya say its effects are like drinking loads of strong coffee?"

"Yeah."

"Well then, no wonder, that would get your heart pumping, wouldn't it? I mean coffee is full of caffeine, that can make people sweat, get the shakes and feel really panicky."

"I guess so, it could be that; I mean I haven't eaten either, maybe that's got something to do with it."

"Exactly; look, you've calmed down a bit already, just by talking about it. Take it easy for a while, and then try a bite of your sandwich. Having something in your belly will only help, food is the best thing, it'll sort you out. Right, I am popping back downstairs, make sure your brother's not nicking Pip's dinner! You'll be fine, love, I'll let you rest and pop in on you in a bit. Just shout if you need me, okay?"

"Okay, thanks, Dad, thanks."

It must be the effects of what I have taken. Dad's words have helped a little, I mean if Benzo Fury is full of caffeine, like coffee is, it's not a surprise that I am feeling so strange. I keep hold of that thought, I take some comfort in thinking about the causes of my feelings and the reaction on all my senses the drug has caused.

I take a small bite of my sandwich and instantly regret it; the soft bread and tuna filling only cause me to purge, I swallow it quickly and struggle to keep it down.

"How's your dinner?"

"Lovely, still a bit full from breakfast though, Dad."

"Yeah, full tummy, Da, Da."

"How's Fran doing, is she getting up?"

"She's getting there, Tom. I don't think she'll be getting up for a while though. How about we all watch a film or something?"

"Yeah, *Lord of the Rings*, please, Dad, please."

"Okay, then, which one?"

"The last one, it has loads of action in it, the final battle for middle earth."

"Fine, you go put it on and I'll tidy up here."

***

I hear the muffled sound of the TV and recognise the title music. Again, not wanting, or feeling able to get up, I drift in and out of my thoughts. School, God, school tomorrow, it seems so near; can I face it? Can I get Tom and Pip ready? Could I get myself ready? Pam, oh, I'll have to face Aunty Pam, she'll be over to look after Pip. Tanya, oh God, how can I face her or Teddy and Robbie? These thoughts overwhelm and confuse me, my head hurts, how can I face tomorrow when I can't even face getting out of bed today? Heart racing again, I hide under my duvet, I want to disappear; please make this stop. I turn onto my front and just try to concentrate on my breathing.

***

"Fran, Fran, come on, love, I am getting a bit worried now. Its six o'clock. I've ironed school uniforms, ready for tomorrow and started to run you a bath. Fran, wake up, come on wake up."

"Ah, okay, Dad, thanks, I... am getting up."

"Good, there's some pizza and salad left for your tea; Tanya called, she asked how you are. She said she's left messages and tried to call; can you call her?"

"Will do, Dad, after my bath."

"Okay, see you downstairs then."

It takes all of my efforts just to get out of my bed. I take a quick glance around my room and feel angry with myself; I've been in bed for most of the day. I pull back my curtains which lets the summer evening sun come streaming in; I squint, and instead of enjoying the still warming rays, the sun feels too bright and too strong on my skin. My thoughts turn to Pip, she must be wondering what's going on, why I haven't been downstairs playing with her, making her favourite food for her or taking her down to the park. I can't stay in my room any longer, I grab some underwear and head for the bathroom.

"Oh, she's up, Pip, who's that getting up?"

"Franny, Fran."

"Yeah, your big sis is up."

"Tom, make your sister a squash, she must be really thirsty."

"Oh, Dad."

"Go on, please."

Dad has put in my favourite bubble bath and laid out a fresh towel, I add some cold water and swish the bubbles around. Ahh, that feels good, I just lay there, not moving, just enjoying the deep soothing hot water and soft, sweet-smelling bubbles. I take my time washing but as soon as I think about getting out, I notice my chest rising and falling, the motion is also moving my stomach in and out of the bath water. I take some deep breaths and push myself up and out of the bath. God, I can't wait for this to stop; what did Dad call it? A come-down. I need this come-down to stop right now. I quickly dry myself and tie my hair up. I roll on some deodorant, put some moisturiser on my face and put on my tracksuit again. Full of nerves, full of fear I head downstairs.

"Hi, love, nice bath?"

"Nice, yeah."

"My Franny, Fran."

"Oh, my little Pip. Oh, I missed you, my love."

"You all right, Fran?"

"Better thanks, Tom."

"I made you some squash, it's on the table there."

"Ta."

"Your tea is in the fridge, love, you can warm the pizza up in the microwave if you want."

"Okay, I'll have it in a bit, what you watching?"

"*Blue Planet Two*, you should see it, love, these creatures that live in the deep; amazing, they're so weird looking."

I settle down on our sofa, with Pip on my lap, the distraction of the TV and having cuddles with Pip is welcomed, I haven't got time to think. Dad and Tom are engrossed watching the TV and, for now, things start to feel quite normal.

"Pam's been over, Fran, she had a nice few hours with Mum. They had a picnic down at Frew's Slope. She said Mum looked well, and your Mum had told her that the new medication was helping. That's some good news, ah?"

"Great... I'll try some of that pizza now."

I only manage to eat one slice of cold pizza and a couple of mouthfuls of green salad. It doesn't go down easily, the pizza base feels like razor blades in my mouth, but the little food I do eat seems to be settling my butterfly filled stomach.

"Dad, you okay to put Pip to bed later? I don't feel great, I may just watch some TV upstairs."

"I can, but you've slept for most of the day, love. I got everything ready for school tomorrow. You've hardly eaten anything; you haven't touched the sandwich I made earlier. I am getting a bit worried, I know you have had a tough night, love, but I've got to get up early for work, and I need to know that you can manage Tom and Pip in the morning, as well as getting yourself off to school?"

"Christ, Dad, how often do I stay in bed? I know it's my fault, I know I've let everyone down. But I don't feel right, if I could just rest some more, then I'll be fine by tomorrow."

"Don't get moody with me, young lady, I've let you sleep it off. By the way, I haven't finished talking about last night yet. Just go to bed, then. I'll sort Pip out, and I will be calling you at breakfast time tomorrow!"

"Fine! 'Night, Pip. See you in the morning little one. 'Night, Tom."

Bloody hell, Dad doesn't understand, I don't understand how I feel but he just adds more pressure. The thought of tomorrow sends me straight into a panic, I rush up the stairs, slamming my door shut behind me. I don't bother undressing, I can't be bothered calling Tanya, I just hide under my duvet again, and with a sense of fear and anger I can't stop thinking about tomorrow.

Chapter 5

I hear the front door being shut and then glance at my phone, five-thirty, two hours yet, I've got two hours yet. I toss and turn, trying to get comfortable, trying to switch my thoughts off. My pillow feels damp under my head, I must have been sweating in my sleep. I pull off my socks and the cold air on my feet feels nice.

I play through in my mind the events of yesterday. As soon as I do, I get that rush of pins and needles, and my chest starts to feel tight. Next, I recognise my fast heartbeat, and beads of sweat form on my forehead. No! Not again, surely this drug is out of my system by now, it's been over twenty-four hours. I try to dismiss my physical feelings but just become annoyed, annoyed with myself, am I going mad? There is something seriously wrong with me.

I consider what I can do, I've got to get Tom and Pip ready, and make them breakfast, give Pip her bath. I can do that, but no way am I going to school. School, the thought sends horrible twinges throughout my body. As I swallow hard, I taste my bitter stale breath. Two hours, I've got two hours before I need to get up.

The next hour or so seems to go so fast. I manage to use the toilet, and my horrible feelings are only heightened when I look at myself in the bathroom mirror. My pupils aren't big and black anymore, but they look tiny, tiny little pin heads. also, there are dark bags under my eyes, and my face looks red and blotchy.

I hear Pip stir in the next room, she often wakes and just talks to herself. I've got to get up. I don't care about getting myself ready, I'm begging to not care about myself at all. I quickly splash some cold water onto my face and then push open Pip's squeaky door.

"Franny, Pip get up? *SpongeBob*, *SpongeBob Adventures*."

"Ha-ha, yes, my love, let's get up then. Did you sleep well, my little Pip? Franny didn't."

"Sleepy all night."

I carry Pip downstairs and pop her down on the sofa as I set-up her DVD.

"There you go, love, *SpongeBob* again!"

I do what I always do; get breakfast ready and tidy the kitchen. I see there is no note on the fridge from Dad this morning, he must be annoyed with me. That upsets me, I know Tom and Pip like to hear me read out Dad's morning message. Anyway, its nearly eight o'clock before I hear Tom get up and head into the bathroom. Pip is happily tucking into her Sugar Puffs and I've decided to make a pot of proper coffee. I am so tired, so ill, it must be some sort of virus, I think to myself.

"Come on, Tom, time is going on!"

"Okay, what's the rush? I am coming."

"Aunty Pam will be here soon, and you haven't had breakfast yet!"

"Coming... why aren't you dressed for school, Fran?"

"Not going, I think I've got some sort of virus or something."

"Oh, does Dad know?"

"No! Not yet he doesn't, I'll call him soon. I told him last night I would get you and Pip sorted, but I don't feel well at all, so I am staying home."

"What about Aunty Pam?"

"What do you mean?"

"Well, what will she say?"

"Uh... I don't know, Tom, she can say what she wants, just eat your breakfast, okay?"

"All right... chill out!"

"Well! I can't worry about what she's going to say, can I? Just eat, I'm going to give Pip her bath."

I normally enjoy bathing Pip, but this morning it's hard work, everything seems to be hard work. I am running late as well and expect a knock on the front door any minute now. Poor Pip, I've rushed her bath, which she loves spending her time in, and now I am quickly dressing her in anything I can lay my hands on.

"Fran… Fran, it's Aunty Pam at the door!"

"Well, open the door then! I'll be a minute or two yet."

"Hi, Aunty Pam, Fran's not going to school today."

"Oh, morning, Tom, why ever not?"

"A virus or something, she said."

"Ah, okay, where is she?"

"Upstairs, getting Pip ready I think."

"Right, you okay getting yourself to school then?"

"Yeah, of course, I've done it before, loads."

"Great, well you better get going then love, it's twenty to nine."

"I'll just grab my bag and coat, and I'm ready."

"I'm off, Fran, see you later, Pip; see you again, Aunty Pam."

"Okay, love, have a good day. Fran… Fran, you okay up there?"

"Won't be a minute, Aunty Pam, just dressing Pip."

Pip is dressed, I am just stalling. Facing Aunty Pam and answering all her questions about Saturday and this morning fill me with dread. That scared, frightening anticipation of the next minute, let alone the next hour, overwhelms me again. I consider shouting for Aunty Pam, just let it all out, a call for help to make sense of how I feel.

I don't though. I pick up Pip, take a deep breath and head down the stairs.

"Hi both, what's up Fran?... Oh, love, what is it? Sit Pip down and come here."

"I want it to stop, I just want it to stop, I'm losing my mind... oh, Aunty, make it stop!"

"What, love?... What is it? Tell me. Pip, your sister's okay. Just watch your DVD, darling. Come in the kitchen, Fran. Have a seat, love, what's going on?

"Oh, I don't know... I feel outside of my body, everything's wrong, everything's... well it's not normal is how I'm feeling."

"Oh, Fran. Come here, give your Aunty a hug."

"It's horrible, it must be a virus, Aunty."

"A virus? What makes you think that, love?"

"I don't know, I've never felt like this before, my heart is going a hundred miles an hour."

"Just breathe, love, calm yourself down, oh God."

"Aunty, I need a doctor, can you call a doctor?"

"Hold on, love, just slow your breathing down first; that's it, deep slow breaths."

"Franny... Franny upset."

"Oh, Pip... I'm okay, just stay in the front room, don't let her see me like this, please."

"Fran's going to be okay, little one, I'll come and see you in a minute, okay? What is it, Fran, did something happen on Saturday night?"

"No, nothing! I drunk some vodka… but I've been feeling weird since Saturday morning, I told Dad then I was feeling really sick."

"Okay, okay, just try and relax, love, we'll sort this out."

"Feel my heart, it's going to explode! I feel faint… I've got to sit down."

"Sit there then, have some water, love."

"I need to lie down, call a doctor… please."

"Oh, Fran, I've got to call your dad."

"No! He doesn't care, please, I'm dying."

"You're not dying, love, you're getting yourself in a right state, your dad needs to be here."

"No, he'll shout, he'll be upset."

"No, he won't, of course your dad cares about you. What about lying down, would that help?"

"I don't know, just make this stop!"

"Oh, love, I would, but I don't know how. Lie down on the sofa for a bit, try that."

"No, no, Pip."

"Pip's all right love. Have a lie down on your bed, then."

"Yeah… I'll try."

Aunty Pam reaches for her phone.

"Frankie, you've got to come home, Fran's in a right state, I am really worried."

"Oh shit, what do you mean, what's happened?"

"She's hysterical, something about a virus, she wants a doctor, Frankie."

"Christ, what's going on?"

"I don't know, do I! Just get home, Frankie, this is scaring me."

"Okay, I can't just get there like that, can I? I'm right in the middle of my round up in Exeter; let me sort something out, and I'll call you right back, okay?"

"Okay, sorry, Frankie, but you needed to know. Fran's really upset; I've never seen her like this."

"Yeah, okay, it's not good, thanks, Pam. I'll be as quick as I can."

God, there's something seriously wrong with me, my thoughts don't seem to belong to me, I mean it's peculiar; for a split second I see myself, watch myself outside my own body, it's like not belonging to anything. Every thought is processed a million times before my mind responds to it. I sink, I drown into my mind.

There's a hum, a ringing sound that surrounds me, it's not in me, it's just hovering around me. I lie still, motionless. I am powerless, it just continually washes all over me.

Numb, uncomfortably numb, I can't move, I don't want to move, someone needs to take care of me, someone must explain how, why. Is this the end? Is this how Mum felt when she decided to end it all?

What would be left behind? How could anyone understand? Pip, Pip would miss me, Tom would lose it for sure. Dad couldn't cope, and Mum would never leave that place. Maybe that's for the best, what good can come from this?

"Fran, can I come in? I've brought you some more water. Fran, you awake? I am coming in."

Come in, I am asleep, you'll never know that I am not. Rest the glass on my bedside table, look at me, feel for me, then leave. I am going, I can't stop that now, this feels like the end.

***

"Pam, I'm on my way; how is she?"

"Oh, Frankie, she's upstairs, her eyes are closed but I don't think she is really sleeping. She was hysterical just a moment ago, so resting, just having some quiet time is a good thing, right?"

"I guess so, give me forty minutes or so, and I'll be home."

"Okay, don't drive like a mad man, be careful, and I'll see you soon."

Aunty Pam replaces the phone and turns her attention towards Pippa.

"Right, little Pippa, what shall we do? Shall we do some colouring or watch some TV?"

"Colours, colouring book, please."

"Okay, go grab your book and pens then."

**

Amongst my scattered thoughts and unclear images, one image overrides all, the image of my mum, just lying there, motionless, lifeless even. Why Mum? How desperate would you need to be to do that? Did she feel like I do now? Confused, numb, unable to make any sense of this. What about our family, how could you leave our family that way?

Did you even think about the aftermath? Who would find you. It could have been Tom. Poor Tom can't talk about what happened because he doesn't know. I know; I found you. Selfish, a selfish thing to do, Mum. I feel I'm seeing clearly for the first time since Mum's suicide attempt, even in this suffocating, debilitating coma I am enduring. Nothing can be the same after that day, I've seen an ending, not a future. God, just let me comfortably slip away, I don't want to think anymore.

**

"That's a lovely colour, darling, is that an elephant? An elephant with shoes on!"

"Yeah, elephant with shoes on, silly elephant."

"Ha-ha, yeah, very silly elephant."

"Oh, that's your dad calling. Hi, love, you nearly home?"

"Not far, I just wanted to check on you all."

"Well, she's still upstairs, Frankie. Me and Pip are fine, just doing some colouring. I've never seen Fran like that though, it reminded me of Launa, that's what scared me."

"Oh, don't say that Pam; it's what she took on Saturday night, some bloody legal high stuff, I didn't say anything because I knew you would only worry."

"What stuff? Christ, Frankie, shall I call a doctor then?"

"No, no, just wait for me to get back, I'm only ten minutes away."

"Okay."

"Right, little one, let's put the kettle on, Dad's coming home."

"Yeah, da, da home."

Frankie returns home.

"Hello, Pam, you okay? Any movement upstairs?"

"No, I've literally just popped my head in, and she's in exactly the same position as before."

"Da, da, you're home."

"Hello, my little orange Pip, I know Dads' home. You been colouring with Aunty Pam?"

"Yeah, elephant with shoes on."

"Wow, that's different, show me, love."

"What's this stuff she's been taking, then?"

"Oh, some legal high shit, Benzo something, it's a stimulant, like speed I guess."

"God, who gave her that?"

"I've got a pretty good idea; I'll deal with him later."

"Who?"

"Tanya's boyfriend, Teddy Newcombe. You know him, he lives up on Tawton Heights, his dad's a right wheeler dealer. Bob, Bobby Newcombe."

"Oh yeah, I know them, his wife drives that white sports thing."

"Yeah, that's right, loads of money from somewhere. Anyway, forget about that for now, what happened earlier?"

"Well, I got here just after eight-thirty, Tom was almost ready, and he told me that Fran was staying home, some sort of virus, he said. So, I hurried Tom up and he was out the door by quarter to nine. I shouted up for Fran, and she came down with Pip in her arms. As soon as I asked her what was going on, she just broke down. She started crying, not making much sense."

"Oh, bloody hell, I knew she was feeling rough, but I thought it was just the effects of the vodka, and that shit."

"Well, I didn't know about that then, I mean, I knew about the vodka, but not the drugs. I tried to comfort her, but she became hysterical, breathing really hard, she kept saying something about a virus, and could I call a doctor."

"A doctor, I'm not sure about that. I mean if it's just a come-down, do we want a doctor involved?"

"Ah, I don't know, Frankie, if you had seen her, she said she felt like she was going mad!"

"Well, we all feel like that sometimes, don't we?"

"I guess so, but it's not something a fourteen-year-old should be saying, is it?"

"No... no, it's not. What can we do then?"

"Well, she's resting for now, so let's just wait, wait and see, see what she's like when she wakes up."

"Yeah, yeah, I guess so, I'll just put my head in and see her I think."

"Okay, I'll make us a cuppa. Have you eaten?"

"I have, we always have a breakfast roll on a Monday, three pound fifty from Greasy Pete's on the city road. Bacon, sausage, two eggs, mushrooms and black pudding; bloody gorgeous."

"Sounds like a heart attack waiting to happen! You fancy a cuppa?"

"Lovely, ta, Pam."

"You want a milky tea, Pip?"

"Please, Pam, Pam."

I hear footsteps on the stairs, the thud, thud sounds heavy, and I wonder if it is my dad. What's he doing home? What's going to happen now? I stay deadly still as my door opens, I daren't look. It is my dad, I can smell tobacco, I can smell that cat piss smell. I suddenly struggle to stay still; I am pretending to be asleep and then doubt that my Dad is falling for that. My eyelids are flickering uncontrollably, how do you pretend to be asleep? If Dad just listened to my fast breathing, surely he would be aware that I am faking it? He stands in my doorway for what seems like an age, I let out a big gasp as I hear my door shut behind him.

"She still asleep, Frankie?"

"Not sure to be honest, I mean she's lying flat on her back, but her eyes were flickering, and I could see her rapid breaths under the duvet. You know what Fran's like when she sleeps; remember Launa always saying that Fran 'cuddles her duvet, the duvet doesn't cuddle her'? Well since she was a little girl, she's always slept like that."

"Yeah, I remember, but if she's resting, well that's okay, isn't it?"

"I'm worried, Pam, there's so much going on. It's so bloody hard on them all. Fran especially, I think. I mean she's been such a rock, looking after Tom and Pip, I've put too much on her. She does so much, she should be enjoying herself, not putting up with all of this. Sorry, Pam, you've had to put up with all this shit too, you know I couldn't cope without your help, don't you?"

"Oh, Frankie, you know I am here, I am here for all of you. We never really know how things are going to turn out, do we? My sister is dear to me, I love her to pieces. I never saw that happening. We talked, but she never gave me any signs she was that ill. Maybe she did, but I didn't sense them. You are doing so well, the kids are doing well, I know Fran has taken it the hardest. She's going to, she found her mum, she thought her mum was dead. Oh my God, I can't imagine how that must have felt."

"I know, I can't change that though, can I? All I've focused on, concentrated on since then, is getting Launa home, getting her well again. That's got to be the best thing, hasn't it? I mean the kids need their mum, I miss my wife, there's got to be hope, hasn't there? If not, what is the point? What is the point of me working seventy hours a week just to pay our mortgage, the bills, and treat the kids to what they want? If Launa can't come home Pam, well, I don't know what's left?

"I see it in Fran, I see that look in her eye, just like her mother. She's not happy, it must be like a ton weight pressing down on her, how the hell has it come to this? She's a child, my first child and I've let her, let them all down."

"Frankie, oh love, come here. Jesus, why is it like this? Launa's doing so much better, yesterday

I could really see a change in her. It's not just this new medication, it's something deeper than that. I can see my sister again, there's life in those big brown eyes. She is more positive. She talked about all of you yesterday, she's looking forward to seeing her home again, yes, her home, Frankie. She knows it's where she belongs, she wants to come home."

"I hope so, Pam, I don't know if I can do this without her."

"I know, love, come on, let's have a seat in the front room with Pip. She's so good, Frankie, so bright. Look at her colouring, it's so precise, I think we may have a little artist in the making."

***

A scary realisation enters my mind, Dad is home because of me, because of how I was with Aunty Pam. Every thought I have seems to produce a physical response, my stomach is turning over and over, which makes me swallow hard, and when the ringing in my head gets louder my heart pumps faster.

A rush, an overwhelming rush that begins in my toes forces its way up through my body towards my head, this is it, I am dying.

"Dad! Dad! Dad! Help!"

"Oh God, that's Fran. Fran, I'm coming, I'm coming. What love? What is it?"

"I'm dying, I'm dying, Dad, I can't breathe! Help me."

"Love, you're not dying, it's a panic attack, I think it's a panic attack; just breathe, remember, just like yesterday."

"No, no, I am going, there's something inside me, virus…"

"Okay, love, okay. Shall I call a doctor? Is that what you want, love?"

"I don't want the doctor… no."

"Pam! Call the doctors, call them right now."

"Doing it."

"Hold my hand, Fran, concentrate on holding my hand."

"Make it stop… it's got to stop."

"We will, I'll make it better love, I am going to make it all better."

***

"Hi, yes I am calling about my niece, Franny Goode, she needs a doctor."

"Okay, do you want to make an appointment?"

"I'm not sure, she's hysterical, something is very wrong."

"Have you called the emergency services?"

"No, you are my first call, someone needs to see her, I don't know what's wrong, can you please send someone?"

"Okay, I need you to calm down, has there been some sort of accident?"

"No."

"Is there any bleeding?"

"I don't know, hang on, she's upstairs with her dad."

"Frankie, I'm on the phone with the receptionist."

"Come upstairs, Pam, and give me the phone."

"I'll just take the phone up to her dad, one second."

Hi, it's Frankie, Frankie Goode, Fran's dad. My daughter's in one hell of a state, she needs a doctor, now!"

"Okay, I appreciate that this is distressing, but I need to know some details, as soon as that's done, the quicker we can get see to your daughter."

"Okay, sorry, I… just don't know what to do."

"That's fine, what is your daughter's name and date of birth?"

"Franny Goode, eighth of the tenth, two thousand and four."

"Who is her GP?

"Doctor Coakley."

"Okay, is that your daughter I can hear in the background?"

"Yes, she's hysterical, she's been feeling rough since Saturday."

"Okay, what's your address and postcode please, Mr Goode?"

"Twenty-two, Oak View, Tawton, EX4 1PP."

"Thanks. Is your daughter bleeding?"

"No, no, you don't understand, there's not been an accident, I would have rung for an ambulance if there was I think she's having some sort of a panic attack, a massive panic attack. I thought seeing a doctor would be best, I don't know. What can I do?"

"Can you bring her to the surgery?"

"Yes, of course; what, come down, right now?"

"Yes, if you can, I'll let Doctor Coakley know, just come to reception and she'll be seen straight away."

"Oh, thank you, thank you, I'll be as quick as I can, thanks again."

"No problem, see you soon."

"You hear that, Fran? We're seeing a doctor, seeing Doctor Coakley, he's going to see you straight away."

"I can't, Dad, I can't leave here, I can't move!"

"Yes, you can, love, the doctor's going to help sort this out, we've got to go."

"Yeah, come on, Fran, honestly, love, it's for the best, you'll see the doctor and he'll make some sense of this."

"I don't want to see anybody, just leave me alone... go!"

"We're not leaving you, love, no way, not in this state. I think you are having a panic attack, it will pass, but you need to see the doctor."

"Panic! Panic attack! It's not that, it's a virus, there's something wrong with my insides."

"Well, maybe; let's see the doctor then, he could tell us, couldn't he? Let him take a look at you, love, I'm taking you, Fran, that's the end of it."

"Oh, Frankie, is she able to go?"

"What? Fran's got to go, Pam, for fuck sake, you can see for yourself she needs a doctor. You okay staying here with Pip?"

"Yes, of course, don't get mad with me, Frankie, just get going then if you're going."

"Fran, I'll carry you if I need to, but we are going, we are going right now!"

"No, Dad, I won't come."

"Don't do that, Frankie, you'll hurt her for god sake, you can't pick her up like that. Lift her like a fireman's lift, not under her arms."

"God! What can I do then, Pam? The doctor's waiting."

"I know, but you can't force her."

"I'm not forcing her... I just need to get this sorted, I can't see her like this... what the hell do you think I can do?"

"Fran, love, your dad wants the best for you, you know that, don't you? I think seeing the doctor is for the best, but you need to agree to that, the doctor will help."

"Fine, fine take me then, they won't understand; I won't speak though, I won't talk."

"Okay, that's fine, let's just see when we get there."

"Pam, sorry, I didn't mean to snap at you, seriously I can't go through this again."

"I know, its fine, just get Fran down there. It's not like Launa, love, it's not like that. Fran will be okay, you'll see."

***

I can't pretend to be asleep anymore, can I? That ship has sailed, I took some comfort in hiding, enjoyed feeling invisible. Now I am on show, laid out bare, in the reception-come-waiting room at my doctor's surgery.

"Mr Goode, I spoke to you on the phone, and this must be Fran?"

"Yes, thanks, thanks for seeing us so soon."

"No, no problem. Doctor Coakley has a patient with him at the moment, but you'll see him next. Just take a seat and he'll come out and call for Fran."

"Okay, thanks. Let's sit here, love, it won't be long."

"Oh, Dad, everything's wrong, I feel faint, lightheaded, I can't stop sweating."

"Just hold on, my love, grab my hand, remember the breathing we did earlier, just try that, the doctor won't be long."

"Dad, are you going to mention the drugs?"

"I hope not to, it'll be out of your system by now, I guess, but it depends on what the doctor asks, won't it?"

I sense that the whole room is looking at me, staring towards me, I turn my head from side to side, unable, unwilling to make eye contact with anybody. The doctor will take some blood and tell me it's a rare virus, he'll give me something to make me feel normal again, a pill, or maybe a course of antibiotics. He doesn't need to know about that legal high stuff. Dad will tell him that I've been feeling ill all weekend, he'll mention my mum's mental health and how her planned return home is causing us all stress. Dad may well tell the doctor about the vodka, but he'll also make it sound like I've learnt my lesson and won't be doing that again.

A tall slender lady pushes open the double doors which are opposite us. "Franny Goode, please."

"Come on then, love, let's see what the doctor says."

Through the double doors is a wide corridor with rooms either side, the doctor stops at the last door on the right and asks us both to come in.

"Hi, both, have a seat."

"Thanks, Doctor."

"How can I help."

"Well, I'm not sure how much the receptionist has told you, but Fran's not feeling well at all. She says that her heart is racing uncontrollably, her breathing is really fast, and she can't stop sweating."

"Okay... well, our receptionist gave me a brief explanation of your recent phone call. It seems that you, Fran, are in some distress? That your heart rate is elevated, and you're having problems breathing? Do you want to tell me about that? When did it start?

My mouth suddenly becomes dry, I try to swallow but I can't without any saliva on my tongue.

"Fran, answer the doctor please, Fran. I'm sorry, Doctor, Fran hasn't really said much since I got home."

"Okay, so let's put it another way then, what made you call the surgery this morning, Mr Goode?"

"Um, well, I was at work when I got a phone call from my wife's sister Pam, she looks after my youngest while I am at work. This was just after nine o'clock this morning. Pam told me that Fran was at home and had become hysterical. She was breathing really fast and not making any sense, and that I should come home right away."

"Right, okay. Fran, can you remember any part of that?"

"Fran, for God's sake answer the doctor!"

"It's okay, Mr Goode, Fran doesn't need to answer that. Fran, do you mind if I examine you? Take your blood pressure, temperature and listen to your heart?"

"She won't talk, Doctor, she's not well, she's not well at all, is she?"

"Well, I am sure it's something we can get to the bottom of, Mr Goode."

"Fran, I'm just going to take your blood pressure, okay? That means I'm going to strap this material around your upper arm, it doesn't hurt."

"Okay."

"Great, you'll feel a little pressure on your arm, that's all."

"Okay."

"Fran, I can hear your breathing is quite fast, try to take some deep breaths in through your nose for me. That's it, nice and slowly. Fantastic, your blood pressure is as it should be. Can I now listen to your heart, please?"

"Yeah."

"Lovely, okay, just unbutton your top for me now, so I can rest the stethoscope over your heart, it's going to feel a little cold that's all."

"Okay, thanks, Doctor."

"Great, that's fine, a little fast, but I think that's down to you being here and feeling a little nervous about that."

"Fran, I want to take your temperature, just open your mouth and I'll pop a thermometer under your tongue. It'll just take a few seconds."

"Oh, my mouth is so dry."

"Just let me pop this under your tongue, shall I get you some water then?"

"Yes, please."

"Just a few more seconds... great, that's all done, here's your water."

I gulp the small plastic cup of water down in one, it tasted warm but still refreshed my mouth.

"Fran, any headaches, or muscle pains?"

"No, nothing like that."

"Great, well, that's all fine, Fran, you seem to be a healthy young woman."

"I don't feel that healthy, Doctor. I just want to feel normal again, I don't feel right, is it a virus?"

"Um, a virus, well, we can take some blood samples, but, Fran, taking some blood now...

today, won't give us an instant diagnosis, you understand that? When we take blood, the samples are sent to a laboratory. They scan the blood for numerous irregularities, such as lack of iron, low proteins, or weak liver function. Fran, in my opinion a virus seems very unlikely in your case. Most viral symptoms will produce a much higher than average temperature, even a rise in your blood pressure. You said you haven't had any headaches?"

"No, no headaches."

"Suffering from chills, or feel dehydrated?"

"No, I don't think so, but I can't eat anything, and can't stop sweating."

"Okay, it can be a bit confusing, Fran, but the loss of appetite, the sweating, these could be symptoms of some sort of anxiety issue. Yes, a virus could make you have a loss of appetite, and make you sweat more, but in my opinion, considering your other symptoms, like faster heart rate, a shortness of breath and sweating, points me towards an anxiety problem."

"Oh, what, nerves you mean? I feel so strange though, so ill, it's hard to explain."

"I know, it's difficult to explain; like I say, with your heart rate being quite fast, and your obvious distress at the moment, I think it's more than likely to be a nervous or anxiety issue. Have you had any of these feelings before, Fran? Like your heart beating faster, feeling faint, or a shortness of breath?"

"Fran's never been a nervous type of child, Doctor. If anything, Fran's been the opposite. Fran has such a fearless competitive streak."

"Well, I have felt anxious before, Dad. I mean my stomach always feels sickly before a swimming race, and my mouth goes really dry, but that's normal isn't it? That's just nerves."

"Exactly, that is a great example, Fran, of how normal levels of anxiety work. So, when you are getting ready to start a race, say, that feeling of anxiety is entirely normal, your muscles will tense, your adrenaline levels increase, readying yourself for the starting gun or whistle. This is what makes us compete, makes us go faster. Does that make sense?"

"I think so."

"Okay, well think of it another way then, just crossing the road produces a higher level of anxiety, your body reacts naturally to that, it realises, and understands how dangerous the road might be. We all get anxious; it helps us avoid potentially dangerous or harmful situations."

"Yeah, I get that, I think, but why am I feeling anxious all the time then? I mean earlier, when I was lying in bed, I felt that I was dying, I thought I was dying."

"Well, that's hard, Fran, obviously. Look, that feeling, or thought, which is very distressing, is a very common symptom whilst suffering from an anxiety attack. Anxiety often makes us think the worse. For example, Fran, if your heart is racing, your first thought might be that it's because of a heart problem. But, in truth, it's because the adrenaline is surging through your body when it's not needed. I mean, you're lying in bed, not crossing a road. So, the release of adrenaline produces various physical and mental responses. Like we said earlier, your heart rate quickens as the adrenaline is pumped through your body. That causes pins and needles from head to toe, you start to sweat, there's a shortness of breath and you can feel lightheaded. All of those symptoms, Fran, would make you believe that there is something very wrong. But believe me, I've been a doctor for over twenty years now and I've never encountered anyone dying from an anxiety attack."

"You see, love, the doctor thinks its anxiety, you've been through so much, love, over the last six months. We can sort this out. Doctor, we can sort this out, can't we?"

"We can; look, I think as your family doctor, the situation with Fran's mum, Launa, is obviously something that needs addressing. I guess that, well, put it this way, that the whole episode is a major cause for concern for all of you, and maybe Fran needs to talk some more about how that situation has affected her."

"That makes a lot of sense, Doctor. Fran, that makes a lot of sense, doesn't it?

"I don't know, I just want to feel normal again."

"Look, there's a lot we can do, Fran. Since you've been here, and you may not have even considered this, but in the time that you have been here you have noticeably calmed down, you have talked openly, and you have been able to answer some pretty difficult questions. Now compare that against how you were feeling just a few minutes ago, and I hope that you can realise that there is always something that can be done. Sometimes just talking about our feelings is a great help."

"Okay, it's a lot to take in, I know. I want to give you some literature about coping with anxiety. This booklet just answers some basic questions concerning anxiety, also let's make an appointment for you to come and see me, well let's say, in four days' time. So, for this coming Friday, okay?"

"Thanks, Doctor, what about going to school? Should Fran just go back to school?"

"Well, I think that would be best, yes. Maybe have tomorrow off, I mean that's up to the both of you. It's obviously been a tough day or so for you, Fran, so maybe just rest tomorrow and take some time to read through the booklet. You could start to try some of the relaxation techniques before heading back to school. Fran, look, continuing with your everyday routine is a very important thing. You'll be surprised how by just doing the everyday things can help, like mixing with your friends, attending school, doing your swimming."

"Okay, I'll try."

"Great, take this booklet and have a read when you have some quiet time, Fran. And please don't hesitate to contact the surgery if you need to."

"Thanks."

"See reception and make an appointment for Friday, just tell the receptionist I've asked to see you on Friday. She'll fit you in."

"Thanks, Doctor, thanks for your time, we both appreciate it; Fran, say thanks."

"Thanks, Doctor, see you soon."

"No problem, that's what I'm here for, Fran; it's going to be fine, just have a rest, and take a look at that booklet when you can, and don't forget, please don't hesitate to contact me if you need to, okay?"

"I will, bye."

We head back down the corridor towards reception, my head is spinning with a million thoughts none of which I properly understand.

"Hello again, could I make an appointment for my daughter, please?"

"Of course."

"Doctor Coakley said to see her on Friday, if that's okay?"

"That's fine, just let me take a look. And it's for your daughter you said, yes?"

"That's right, Franny Goode."

"Fine, how about Friday morning at eleven thirty?"

"Great, that's great."

"Okay, I'll just write that down for you."

"Thanks, I don't think we'll forget though."

"There we go, all done, so that's Doctor Coakley, this Friday at eleven thirty."

"Thank you, see you then, bye now."

***

"Oh, love, well done. That must have been hard. You feeling a bit better after that?"

"I don't know, Dad. Confused, not better. Is this like what Mum went through?"

"Oh, Fran, it's not like that, your mum suffered from depression, that's why she saw Doctor Coakley. It's not the same love. Doctor Coakley thinks you're suffering with anxiety. I mean, she would know, wouldn't she? Those feelings that you're having are down to feeling anxious, we can sort that out, love. It's not a virus, or something like that, so that's positive, isn't it?"

Positive, positive, I feel like I am losing my mind, just like Mum; and Dad says positive. He doesn't understand, I don't understand. Doctor Coakley has made some sense of it, but now, having left the doctor's I feel more confused than I did before.

"Yeah, I'm glad it's not a virus, and he made some sense of it, Dad, yeah."

"Good, let's get you home, unless you fancy going somewhere?"

"Going where?"

"I don't know, are you hungry? I could treat you to a breakfast at McDonald's, we could go to the drive-through in Okement, then take it up to the moor?"

I feel obliged to say yes, even though my first instinct is to say no. I understand that my dad is just trying to do something nice, something we haven't done together for such a long time.

"Sounds good, Dad, I do feel a little bit hungry."

"I bet you do, love. I'll give Pam a quick call, and then we can head off, she'll be wondering what's going on."

Dad talks to Aunty Pam and explains what has just happened. Dad's explanation over the phone sounds positive, but I suddenly feel like a sideshow, a passenger without a voice. Is that it, then? The doctor, after ten minutes or so, has decided that I am suffering from anxiety, that I'm mental. She's handed me some booklet and told me to just carry on. Go to school, mix with friends, do what's "normal". Well, normal seems to be a long way off, I can't help but think that being normal is not what's in store for me.

My mum's suicide attempt suddenly flashes in my mind, then the thought of Mum coming home sends shudders down my spine. An unpleasant rush surges throughout my body again; it's happening again, am I becoming ill, like Mum? Am I mentally ill? How is Mum going to react after hearing about today? What will my friends at school think? How will Tom and Pip cope?

"Right, Pam asked if we could get her and Pip a McFlurry? She didn't say which flavour, but Pip loves that mint one doesn't she?... Fran, you okay?"

"Oh, yeah, sorry, Dad, I was miles away. The mint one, yeah, that's her favourite, I think Aunty Pam likes the caramel one. Do they serve ice-cream for breakfast though, Dad?"

"Good question, I'm not sure love. We'll soon find out."

The journey to Okement feels painfully slow. It's not down to heavy traffic or anything like that, and it's not because there is an uncomfortable silence between me and my dad. Dad and I have been talking, but just talking about everyday things, like the weather, what we fancy from McDonald's, or if Tom will forgive us for going to McDonald's without him. The journey feels slow because I am lost, stuck with one thought, the thought of that day, five months or so ago, a day which I often relive in my mind, but have never really talked about with anyone.

Dad is puffing away on his roll-up and I am just lost in my thoughts. The doctor has made some sense of how I feel, but I'm still so confused; every thought I have seems to produce that fearful, panicky feeling throughout my whole body. He mentioned talking about Mum and her "situation". What is there to talk about? I found Mum, I found her, I may have even saved her life. The doctors in Accident and Emergency had later explained to Dad that my mum was lucky to be alive. She had taken such a large number of anti-depressants, that if she hadn't been found when she was, she would have died. When Dad told me that just a few days later, I felt proud at first, proud that I had found her, that I, who had sensed that there was something very wrong that day, had then felt the need to sprint home, run like I have never run before, to, as it turns out, save my mum's life.

As those painful first few days passed by, that initial feeling of pride started to feel more like a heavy pressure. A pressure from all around, an unseen heavy weight that was forcing down onto my skull, and then spilling its forceful pressure out into my brain; a pressure that consumed my every movement and thought. The reality was overwhelming; if I had just strolled home in a daydream that day, or if I had just decided to spend some time chatting with Tanya, then my mum would have died.

Why had Dad told me that? Did he think it would help? I've never been able to ask him; the weight of those unanswered questions still hang above me, like a black cloud. That overwhelming feeling of fear and uncertainty has returned, it's not the same weight as before, but a deeper, darker, all-consuming pressure that I can't get rid of, that I can't take.

"Are we going to tell Mum about me seeing the doctor today, Dad?"

"Ah, Fran, I really don't know... I think we must, don't you?"

"It's going to really upset her, you know?"

"Yeah, it will be upsetting, but she's got to be told, I mean how could we keep that from her? God, I don't want you to have to worry about that though, love."

"Well, worry is what all of this is about, isn't it? That's what the doctor thinks."

"Yes, yes is it, love, I feel so helpless though, Fran. I just want you all too be well; I want your mum home... I want you to feel better, I want you,

Tom and Pip to feel excited about having your mum home. Oh, don't cry, love, you'll get me started and we'll never be able to stop."

"Oh… Dad, it's so hard, I can't explain it!"

"I know, I know it's so bloody hard love, we can sort it though, the doctor thinks talking about everything is a good idea, I mean you can talk to me about anything, you know that."

"I know, Dad, but I can't really explain how I'm feeling, I… I can't put it into words, I mean."

"Yeah, I understand that, so maybe talking to Mum about how you feel would be a good thing? I mean she's more likely to be able to understand what's going on than me."

"Oh, I don't know, Dad, I think it would be too much for Mum right now."

"Maybe, let's just see how things go this week, then? Take tomorrow to rest, get that shit out of your system and read through that booklet the doctor gave you. You'll feel better, Fran, you'll see."

Poor Dad, he's just trying to keep everything together, that's all he's ever tried to do, he doesn't want to make any big decisions, I understand that. Dad wants what's best for everyone, but I know, I sense it even, that when Mum hears about my visit to the doctor's it will destroy her. The news of my own mental health problems will set her back, make her confront her own raw, mental fragility, and that will make her feel very ill again.

I can see it now; it's clearly laid out in front of me. That's it! A moment of clarity, I think to myself, the whole last six months have been building to this. Just the thought of my mum coming home has brought up so many feelings and fears, that I've unknowingly just buried, hidden, locked away. That image, that image of my mum lying unnaturally stiff on our sofa, her limbs twisted and distorted in a painless sleep, that terrible gut-wrenching moment when I found my mum is imprinted onto my brain, how could it not be?

Chapter 6

The next few days have come and gone with me existing in some sort of strange reality, between a living nightmare and a weird kind of clarity, which becomes more and more blurred and distorted depending on my feelings and thoughts.

Going to school on Wednesday was terrible, I thought I was going to faint when I first saw Tanya and her brother across the road from me and Tom, I don't know how I managed to cope with how I was feeling and thinking. It seemed that I had to think about what I was going to say before I actually said it, then I would replay and rethink how that would sound to others, all this happened in a split second but it felt like I was having a long conversation with myself before I actually managed to say anything.

After me and Dad had sat on the moors eating and drinking our McDonald's breakfast and coffee, I had spent the Monday hiding away up in my bedroom and feeling really scared about everything.

Dad would pop his head in every hour or so and ask if I was okay. I felt smothered by his continued presence, my head started to hurt, and I felt suffocated by my panicky thoughts. My bedroom suddenly seemed smaller somehow, the walls were closing in, and I felt claustrophobic, unable to escape from my own self-made prison.

So, on Monday evening I just tried to relax, but every time I thought about the next day, the next hour or going back to school on Wednesday, I felt more and more anxious. My phone was full of unanswered messages, all from Tanya. I finally replied at about ten o'clock that evening, *Sorry T, not well at all, will tell u more Weds, when I'm back, cu then, normal time/place xx Fran*. Tanya, didn't reply, and that just heightened my anxiety, I drifted in and out of a restless, uncomfortable, sweat-covered sleep for the rest of that night.

For a split second when I woke up the next morning I felt fine, normal even, but as I lingered in bed that fearful cloud slowly reappeared. The thought of having a whole day at home, which would normally be great, suddenly felt like a long, lonely and scary prospect. At first my arms and legs began to tingle, then my heart started racing again. I took some deep breaths and had to really force myself to get out of my warm bed. I needed to do things quickly, *Just get Tom and Pip sorted then I can go back to bed*. That would not give me any time to really stop and think. I brushed my teeth in a matter of moments and then washed my face with just cold water. I glanced at myself in the mirror, but then quickly turned away.

Tom was quiet over breakfast, he was slowly shovelling in his coco rice and taking care not to spill any of the chocolaty milk onto his school tie. I guess he could tell I was in no mood for his normal early morning, hyperactive behaviour. Pip was quiet too, but I think that was just down to her feeling tired, she couldn't stop yawning, and nearly fell back to sleep in her bowl of Sugar Puffs. I had to keep calling her name out just to keep her awake. I made some toast for myself but couldn't face more than one or two mouthfuls.

Dad had left a note on the fridge, but unlike his normal humorous words it read, "Morning all. Fran, Pam is coming over at 7.30 this morning to give you a hand with the kids. Try and have a good day, get some rest, Love you all Dad xx."

It was just after seven when I had read Dad's note. I felt not only rushed, which I hate, but slightly angry and annoyed by his words. I made us all a cuppa and started to tidy the front room. Tom was slurping his tea, and Pip was happily moving her Sugar Puffs around her bowl with her fingers, when there was a knock on the front door. *Jesus, its only quarter past seven and Aunty Pam is here already!* Aunty Pam had arrived early, so Tom and Pip were still finishing their breakfast.

"Morning all, lovely sunny morning again, how are we today?"

"Fine thanks," Tom replied, with no warmth at all.

"Yeah, okay I think, Aunty Pam, you didn't need to come over so early, I'm off school today, and Tom and Pip are almost ready."

"Well, I don't mind, love, your dad just thought I might be able to help, that's all. But great, I can see you've got it all covered. I tell you what, let me do the dishes then?"

"Oh, okay, thanks Aunty Pam, that is a big help."

Do I need babysitting? Is that what this is all about. I resented my aunty's early arrival and felt an anger towards my dad that I've never felt before. I left Aunty Pam downstairs to the dishes and quickly got myself dressed, without really caring how I looked. No make-up, just deodorant and a quick brush of my hair. I will be back in bed soon anyway, back to the safety of my room. Tom had his school bag slung over his shoulder by the time I came back down the stairs, and Aunty Pam was in the kitchen putting the dishes away. Pip was still in her chair looking on.

"You all sorted, Tom?"

"Yes, Fran, you always ask me that! Why do you always ask me that?"

"I know, sorry, it's just habit. Have a good day then, see you later."

"Yeah, I'll try to."

Tom was out the door, *in a bit of a strop*, I thought, and now Aunty Pam was seeing to Pip. She was lifting her up from her chair and I noticed a few Sugar Puffs were sticking to her fingers.

"Right, I'm going to take a look at this booklet the doctor has given me, so I'm going up to my room, okay?"

"Okay, Fran, just try and rest though as well, I'm going to take Pip into town soon, do some shopping and then head to the park, so see you in a bit."

"Okay." *Thank God, I can just escape everything and everyone and go to my room.* I stayed dressed but felt tired again. I contemplated looking at my booklet, but instead I got under my covers and shut my eyes.

I woke up confused about what day and time it was. At first it felt like the next day, and everything I remembered about this morning was yesterday. It took me a while to get my bearings, I glanced at my phone and saw it was nearly two o'clock. *God, I've slept loads.* I woke up feeling really dehydrated, so I headed down to the kitchen and made myself a pint of squash.

I turned on the telly and put on Channel 5. There was a black and white family film on, something about a cattle ranch and a railroad company. I still felt really lethargic, so I just crashed out on the sofa and tried to focus on the TV.

I heard Aunty Pam outside, it sounded like she was having a conversation with one of our neighbours. As soon as I heard her voice I felt panic; I quickly got up from the sofa, turned the TV off and scarpered up to my room. My heart was racing and as I sat on the edge of my bed that awful fearful feeling hit my guts again, and I became emotional. *What I'm I doing? Why can't I face anyone? Am I going mad?*

***

I must have spent the next few hours just drifting in and out of sleep, because the next thing I remember is hearing the comings and goings of Aunty Pam; she must have looked in on me because I heard my door being opened. I also heard gunfire and explosions as Tom must have been playing on his Xbox, and finally as I started to come around, I smelt the frying of onions and garlic as Dad cooked our evening meal.

The smell of cooking, which normally would be a welcome one, this time made my stomach turn sickly and produced a moist, bitter taste into my mouth. I swallowed hard to remove the taste and then took a sip of my squash; I considered having a shower, but again just felt so lethargic and unmotivated. I popped to the loo, and Dad must have heard me as I walked across the landing.

"Fran! You having some tea? It's spag bol with grated cheese and garlic bread."

"I don't feel that hungry, Dad... sorry, my stomach feels upset."

"Well, you haven't really eaten much have you, maybe just try a little bit, it may help?"

"Okay, I'll try, give me a minute and I'll be down."

"Okay."

I did feel hungry, but the thought of facing everyone was making me feel more nauseous than the smell of the food. The other frightening thought that consumed me was school tomorrow, as soon as it entered my mind I became anxious again. *Could I do it, could I face Tanya, Teddy, Robbie? Could I even go to school feeling like this? Everyone will see that I'm mad, that I'm mentally ill.*

I tried to eat, I tried to make conversation, but after a couple pieces of garlic bread and a few mouthfuls of spaghetti Bolognese I felt full, and my efforts to get Dad or Tom speaking about anything had failed. I sat at the kitchen table feeling alone and confused. I felt that as Saturday drew nearer, Tom and Dad seemed more and more preoccupied within their own thoughts. *How did they truly feel about Mum's visit? Like me, did they find themselves doubting the idea, and do they really think it's best not to talk about it, not to really say how they feel?*

As I finished the dishes and started to wipe the kitchen table, I felt hot and bothered. I needed to be on my own again, it's for the best, my mind was overwhelmed with horrible, negative thoughts about school tomorrow. *Will people see that I'm mentally ill? Will I faint? Will I have to run away in a panic? Am I going insane?* I made my excuses, told Dad my stomach was still playing up, so I was having a bath and getting an early night. Dad was watching the TV with Tom and Pip, and they all wished me a goodnight, saying it at the same time. *A goodnight; whatever this night brings it's not going to be good one*, I thought.

After my bath, which I thought would relax me, but instead didn't because I spent most of my time transfixed on my accelerated heartbeat, I decided to try and look at the booklet the doctor had given me.

The booklet talked about "anxiety's vicious circle" and how a thought can produce a physical response. That rang true with me because every time I'd had a negative thought there would be a noticeable physical response. The booklet also explained some relaxation techniques, like controlled breathing, so I lay flat on my bed and tried to follow the instructions. At first it felt like it may work, but my confused thoughts just got in the way, I kept drifting off into some weird scary place in my mind, and all I became acutely aware of was how strange and ill I actually felt. I put the booklet down and pulled my duvet above my head, conscious now of how fast and amplified my own breathing and heart rate had become.

***

I woke up at least three times that night, once to go to the toilet, and twice when I was falling or been bitten in a vivid nightmare. It took me what seemed like hours to get comfortable again and drift off.

In the morning, at first I just felt tired; I brushed my teeth, washed my face, got dressed all in some sort of "zombie" state. I didn't fully come around until I was dressing Pip, I think her smile and giggling brought me back to the now. And the now was scary, it was school, I felt raw panic.

Unable to face any food myself I bowled up Tom and Pip's cereals and made us all a cuppa, before I went to my bedroom and tried to collect my thoughts. I thought about pulling a sicky, pretending to go to school, then hiding down by the river for the day, but by the time Aunty Pam had arrived, and Tom had dressed himself, I had managed to find from somewhere a strength to at least try to face the day.

I walked with Tom until he met up with Noah at the junction of Pine Rise and Maple Drive, we didn't say much to each other, and in a way I was pleased. I don't think I could have explained anything to Tom, even if he had asked about the last few days. After Tom and Noah had headed off, I met up with Tanya and Bobby on the opposite side of the road. Tanya seemed off with me, she looked worn out and thinner somehow, we only said a few words, I guess Bobby sensed an atmosphere between us and instead of walking side by side with his sister he had hurriedly walked off in front of us.

"How you feeling, Fran?"

"Like shit, I don't know where to begin, Tan."

"Me too, I'm so sorry it ended up like that."

"I know, but it's my fault; let's just get to school and get this day over and done with."

***

In the first few minutes of my first lesson at school I considered just getting up and leaving, the tightness in my chest was so painful that I convinced myself I was having a heart attack. Only the thought of how I would look, and what people would say and think, stopped me from physically getting up and running away.

At dinner time I met up with Tanya again. She was looking ill, but all her symptoms were down to drinking too much and snorting that bloody Benzo Fury stuff. She looked pale, and for the first time since I've known her she looked rough and untidy, her make-up looked rushed and her normal bright blue eyes seemed darker and heavier. We didn't really say much to each other, but I broke the silence and apologised for not replying to her messages and told her that I had gone to the doctors, and that she had diagnosed me with some sort of anxiety disorder. Tanya hugged me, and said sorry, but I felt no real feeling in her embrace or apology. We left each other that dinner time, both feeling confused and cold towards each other, I think.

My last lesson on Wednesday was maths. I had really struggled to keep it all together but managed to talk myself through most of the day by just concentrating on my breathing, as well as counting numbers in my head when I started to feel really panicky. By the time I got to my final lesson I was feeling pretty worn out and tired of masking all my anxieties. I hate maths, and if I had had any confidence in myself whatsoever, I would have just walked away before the lesson began.

I was sitting next to Stacy Turner and just pretending to concentrate on the assignment when I suddenly felt faint, my whole body started to shake and I was sweating all over, my mouth became so dry and all I could smell was a sweet, sickly perfume. I was just holding on, that's how it felt, my body strained, and I could feel every muscle tense up. *I can't faint, how stupid would I look? Please don't let me faint.*

Stacy could tell there was something wrong with me, she held my arm and then shouted towards Mr Humphreys. "Mr Humphreys, Mr Humphreys, I think there's something wrong with Fran."

I don't think I fainted but the next thing I can remember is being led out of the classroom with Mr Humphreys and Stacy holding me under each arm.

"Let's get you some fresh air, Fran, and then maybe get hold of a first aider to come and have a look at you."

Mr Humphreys sat me down on the nearest bench, which sits just a few yards outside our maths classroom between two large oak trees. I remember taking big deep breaths and by doing that, as well as being out in the fresh air, I started to feel a bit better, my shaking and sweating eased off a little, and my vision started to clear.

I could hear the chit-chat and giggles of my classmates, and when I glanced up towards the classroom windows, I could see everyone staring and pointing at me.

"So sorry, sir, I feel so stupid, did I actually faint?"

"Don't be silly, you've got some colour coming back in your face now, Fran. You didn't faint, you looked like you were going to, but me and Stacy got to you before that."

"Thanks, sir, thanks, Stacy."

"No problem, I could tell you were not right, I could see your pen was shaking as you wrote."

I stayed sitting outside with Stacy and Mr Humphreys, who was on the phone now to our receptionist and first aider, Jane Mayhill. I started to slowly feel better, but I felt so tired all of a sudden, my body ached like it does the day after doing a long and hard swimming lengths session.

"How you feeling now, Fran, any better?"

"Yes, much better, sir, thanks."

"Great, Jane Mayhill is on her way, okay? I am just going to the classroom before there's a riot! Stacey, you okay to stay with Fran until Jane Mayhill gets here?"

"Of course."

"Great, I am just a stone's throw away, shout if you need me."

"Okay, we will be fine, sir."

By the time Jane Mayhill got to us I was feeling more embarrassed than ill. She asked what had happened, took my pulse and gave me a bottle of water. At first, I felt that I could have told her all about this last week, but then I decided it was going to be such hard work to go over everything, especially as I didn't really understand what was going on myself.

Jane sat with me, and she tried to keep me company by talking about the weather and asking if was going on holiday in the summer break. She mentioned something about her planning a trip to Italy with her husband, but I didn't say much in reply, I just wanted to get home and hide under my duvet again.

By the time the end of lesson bell rang I was up on my feet and felt anxious to leave, but Jane insisted that I needed to follow her back to reception to fill out a sickness at school form. Stacy kindly came out of the lesson with my school bag, I thanked her and then followed Jane towards reception, feeling very embarrassed and self-conscious about what had just happened.

After filling in a form at reception, I hurriedly walked out of the school gates. I felt paranoid every time I saw someone, *They're all laughing at me, everyone knows I am mentally ill, I bet the whole school knows that I nearly passed out earlier. I bet it's all over Facebook.*

I quickened my pace as I passed the clock tower and then the Spar. By the time I got to my street I was sweating again, but I shrugged that off as it was a hot day and I was practically running by then. As soon as I reached the front door, I suddenly had a panicky thought, *Did I say I would meet Tom, and walk home with him?* I couldn't remember, but it was too late to do anything about it now anyway.

The house was empty, Dad was doing some overtime and Aunty Pam was probably having her daily walk with Pip. I felt a bit guilty about Tom, and I promised myself that I would apologise and try to explain everything to him later. I dropped my school bag, grabbed a glass of water and made my way upstairs, to the safety of my bedroom.

**

Everyone seemed to arrive home at the same time that day. I heard Tom's voice as he was speaking to Aunty Pam and Pip outside by the front door and then moments later Dad had turned up, I could hear the squeak and rattles of our old beat up Volvo as he reversed into a space near to our house.

I suddenly felt so isolated from everybody, as if I wasn't present somehow. *I'm not telling Dad about earlier, I feel so stupid, and he'll just worry, and go on about it all evening.* Things were just carrying on as normal, but I'm not normal, am I? Not at all normal, not anymore.

"Fran, Franny you upstairs?"

"Yes, Dad, just getting changed."

"Okay, everyone's here."

Everyone's here, I know that. *That's why I'm hiding in my bedroom.* I got dressed into some jogging bottoms and a T-shirt and collapsed onto my bed. I was so tired, tired of feeling anxious, tired of feeling tired, and before I knew it, I was shutting my eyes and drifting away into a fog-filled sleep.

Knock-Knock. "Fran, it's your dad, you okay?"

"Oh… hang on, what time is it?"

"Six thirty, you coming downstairs?"

"Yeah, sorry, just give me a minute, Dad."

"Okay, love, I think Pip's missing you."

Those words cut deep into me from the inside out, my stomach rolled over, and I felt nauseous and hurt. *I can't help how I feel, can I?* But by feeling so ill and being so distant and distracted, have I let Pip down? My own frustration in needing to be isolated from people began to grow into an anger and pain I've never felt before. After five to ten minutes I decided I had to face everyone, so with anger and resentment in my heart and that sickening feeling in my stomach I headed downstairs.

That evening, I spent most of my time with Pip, just playing with her toys on the front room floor. Dad had cooked some sausages and mash and we all sat around the dinner table not saying much to each other. I asked Tom if I had planned to walk home with him after school, but he said that we hadn't.

I wanted to ask Dad if he had spoken to Mum and explained what had happened to me. But, for some reason I just couldn't find the words. I was still angry with him, and soon realised, because of the silence and strange atmosphere around the table, that tonight wasn't a good night to mention it.

When our tea was finished, I washed all the dishes and quickly tidied the kitchen, before making my excuses to return up to my bedroom; I told Dad that my stomach was feeling sickly and I just needed to lay down. But, in my head, I was already planning ahead; I would bunk off school tomorrow, I couldn't face it, no way am I well enough to cope with school, especially after what had happened today. Friday I was off anyway for my eleven thirty appointment with Dr Coakley. So, my plan was to set my alarm for five twenty, fake a stomach bug, and then confront my dad with this just before he left for work.

With my plan fixed in my mind, I got into bed and willed myself to fall asleep without having that awful fearful feeling in my gut and those rapid palpitations of my heart.

***

I was awake just before my alarm went off; *my mind must have sensed the importance of my plan, I guess*. From my bedroom I could hear Dad downstairs in the kitchen, so I headed to the bathroom and without any hesitation I stuck two of my fingers down my throat, I retched a few times, choked a little and then finally started to bring up last night's sausages. Now that I had forced myself to be sick, I couldn't stop being sick, it hurt my face as I retched again and again.

"Fran, Fran, is that you being sick, love?"

"Oh, Dad, yes, my stomach feels really bad, I've been feeling sick since having food last night."

"Ah… love, okay, I've got to go to work now though, Fran, are you going to be okay do you think? Can you manage to sort Tom and Pip out until Pam gets here?"

"I think so, but I can't go to school feeling like this, Dad."

"I know, I get that Fran, I'll call them when I'm at work; just try and get some rest then, okay?"

"Thanks, Dad."

"I'll call later, see how you are."

"All right, speak later."

My plan had worked even better than I had imagined, I didn't even have to face Dad, and he's going to ring the school for me as well, which is so much better, because with Dad ringing it will sound more convincing.

For a brief moment, after I've stopped being sick, I feel pleased with myself, I've managed to escape school. I don't have to face anyone or do anything.

By the time Tom had left for school and Aunty Pam had arrived to take care of Pip, my brief feeling of euphoria had turned into a nagging self-doubt. I began to realise that all I had really managed to do by bunking off school, was to isolate myself even more, and that hiding away from everything didn't really help, and couldn't last.

After watching a couple of hours of some crappy daytime TV, my mind started to go somewhere dark and unwelcoming. At first, I just felt sorry for myself, I wallowed on the sofa about my own desperate, anxious and confusing situation.

Why me? I've tried to keep it all together after Mum's suicide attempt and committal to Park Place; I've cooked, cleaned, done the washing and ironing for everyone, got Tom ready for school, washed and dressed Pip every day. I've really tried hard to concentrate on my schoolwork, especially with my exams just around the corner and I've really trained hard in the pool for my swimming team.

I spent the rest of the day up in bed just fretting about everything, I couldn't switch my mind off. I even felt a bit guilty about lying to Dad. I heard Aunty Pam and Pip come in around midday and felt the need to physically hide under my covers, I didn't want to see anybody, I didn't want to have to think about anything, *just please let me sleep.*

***

I must have slept for hours, because the next thing I remember was hearing Dad and Tom playing football outside. My curtains were open, and the sun's glare was penetrating its warmth onto my feet which were poking out from the bottom of my duvet.

As soon as I came around fully, I felt the now familiar sequence of events begin. Firstly, I became aware of my negative thoughts; that would then make my arms and legs begin to tingle, just like pins and needles. The tingling is an uncomfortable sensation which then later turns into an ache and a feeling of heaviness throughout all of my limbs. Then, I can feel a quickening of my heartbeat, I often just lay on my bed feeling the palpitations with my hand, unable to slow them down, or resist the urge to watch my chest as it rises and falls so dramatically. Finally, my stomach starts to feel strange, it becomes tight and painful, like when you have eaten too much over Christmas. Once that pain and vice-like tightness eases off, my stomach feels nauseous; that feeling stays with me for the rest of the day.

"Fran, you okay? Can I come in?"

I ignored my dad and pretended to be asleep, he called my name again and I heard him slowly push open my bedroom door. He stood there for a while, and I tried to slow my breathing down, as if to convince him that I was fast asleep. Dad left, and quietly pulled the door shut, I heard him as he went down the stairs and then talked to Tom in the hallway. I couldn't make out what was being said but thought it might have been about me. I spent the next hour or so just listening to the noises from outside and the sounds of the muffled voices from the front room. I became convinced everyone was talking about me. I tried to listen hard to hear what was being said, but as I became aware of the quietness all around, all I could hear was the thud, thud of my own heartbeat. I turned over in my bed and sank my head deep into the pillows, feeling isolated, anxious and alone.

Chapter 7

"Love! Dinner's ready, it's on the table, come and get it!" Dad is shouting up the stairs, and Tom joins in by saying, "Come on, sleepy head, it's Dominos, we got you that meatball one, your favourite."

I ignore them both at first, but have woken up feeling pretty hungry, especially now I know that my favourite pizza is sitting in its box on our kitchen table. My mouth becomes wet as I think about the tasty meatballs and the melting cheese. No more than a minute later, someone comes running so fast up the stairs I thought at first it must be Tom, but it isn't, it's Dad, he must have taken two steps at a time.

"Fran, I'm coming in love, want to make sure you're okay."

"All right, come in."

"Hi, love, how you feeling? Still feel sick?"

"A little bit, yeah, I've just slept for most of the day, couldn't do anything else."

"Best thing for you when you're feeling sick. I spoke to the school, and told them you're unwell, some stomach bug I said."

"Thanks, Dad."

"Also, I reminded them about you being off all day Friday because of your doctor's appointment."

"Oh, thanks, Dad, I appreciate that."

"Look, Fran, I know you are going through something here that I don't fully understand, but I love you, you know that. I've left you alone these past couple of days to give you some space, but I am here for you, love, and always will be."

"Oh, Dad, I know, I really do. I can't explain what's going on with me, but I think seeing the doctor again on Friday is only going to help me."

"It will, love. Remember Monday? Just by talking to her then, that seemed to help, didn't it?"

"It did, but Dad, I think the way that I'm feeling has a lot to do with what's happened to Mum. And now, with her coming back to the house on Saturday, I mean I know it's only for a couple of hours, but the last time I saw Mum here in our house was, well, when I found her, wasn't it?"

"Oh, my darling… I never thought about it like that. God, that's awful, love, it never crossed my mind. I feel so stupid, I've just been so wrapped up in trying to get your mum better and having her come back home where she belongs that I didn't think about how it would make you all feel, especially you, Fran."

"It's not your fault, Dad, it's no one's fault. I just needed to say that out loud."

"Well I'm glad you did; shit, Fran, no wonder you've been feeling so anxious, I mean that's a big thing to deal with. God, Fran, what can we do? What can I do?"

"I don't know, Dad, it all feels so complicated, I hate thinking like this, being so negative about it all. I want Mum to be happy and well, of course I do, but I can't feel like this every time I think about Mum coming home. I can't cope with feeling like this, the whole thing is making me ill."

"Oh, love, I know, don't cry, Jesus, why is everything so bloody hard for us?"

Me and Dad hug each other, and even though Dad isn't crying I can sense that he is only just managing to hold back his own tears. I suddenly feel like a parent might do; Dad suddenly feels small, weak and fragile in my arms.

"Dad, listen, I've got the doctors tomorrow, maybe just by talking things through with her, and trying those relaxation techniques will help; she will help, Dad, I know it. I will get better you'll see."

My words seem to have broken down my dad's defences, he starts to cry, and I can feel his body as it uncontrollably starts to shake next to mine. I hold him as tight as I can, we don't talk, we don't need to talk, we understand each other's pain.

***

"Come on, you two! What you doing? Your pizzas are getting cold."

Tom's loud words immediately bring Dad and me back to the now.

"Oh, Fran, I'm so sorry, love, I didn't want you to see me like that. I don't want Tom and Pip to see me like this, love, could you go down to them? Make sure they are okay for me?"

"Yes, of course, Dad, take your time."

I leave my dad in my room and head down the stairs.

"Hey, good to see you, Fran!"

Tom, who is sitting around the kitchen table has a big tomatoey sauce and pepperoni-stained smile.

"Yeah, very funny, Tom; you left any pizza for me then?"

"Loads, I haven't even touched yours, I don't like meatballs anyway."

Tom and Pip are both stuffing slices of pizza into their mouths, the kitchen table seems to be full of opened pizza boxes. Pip's favourite, ham and pineapple, has somehow managed to make its way onto the kitchen floor, and as I look over to Tom, Pip's pizza has miraculously made its way onto his plate as well.

"Yum, yum, Pip, is that tasty, little one?"

"Pinpaple, I love pinpaple, Fran."

"Ha-ha, I know you do, love, looks like your brother does too!"

"No, she gave me a slice, that's all, honest."

"Okay, Tom, whatever you say."

"Where's Dad, Fran?"

"He's coming. He's just in the loo, I think."

I get stuck into my meatball pizza and it tastes lovely, I haven't really eaten much since Saturday morning so the warm slices of my twelve-inch meatball and cheese pizza are going down well. I hear Dad as he shuts his bedroom door and starts to come down the stairs.

"Okay, what's left for your dad then? Tom, have you eaten mine as well?"

"Oh, Dad, no honestly, I've had mine and Pip wanted me to try a slice of hers."

"Really?... Well that's nice of you, Pip, and did your brother give you a slice of his?"

"No, da, da, pinpaple for me."

We all laugh out loud, and for the first time in what feels like a long time I feel happy, normal even. This is what our tea times are normally like, I love just being surrounded by my family, doing what we normally do, just laughing and joking with each other. As I tuck into my second slice of pizza I think, for the first time in days, more positively about the future.

After tea I quickly wash the few dishes we have used, while Dad, Tom and Pip settle down to watch

EastEnders. I hate *EastEnders*, I find it so depressing and dull, so instead I make a fuss of Pip, who I'm certain doesn't consider watching *EastEnders* as an important part of her evening.

"Let's make a tower with all your blocks, Pip."

"Yeah, blocks, my blocks."

We both build our own fragile looking towers and it's not long before mine is falling down.

"Fallen, I win, Franny."

God, Pip hasn't called me Franny for ages, the sound of my full name makes me smile.

"Yes, you win, shall we do it again?"

"Yeah, again, again."

We play on, whilst Dad heads out the front door for a roll-up.

"Is everything okay, Fran?"

"Oh, Tom, I'm not feeling great."

"I thought something was up, I haven't really seen you since Saturday."

"I know, sorry, everything's feels like a bit of a mess for me at the moment; I mean, I feel okay tonight, but the last few days have been pretty terrible."

"Why, what's happened?"

"Oh, Tom, it's complicated, but I think having Mum come home on Saturday has brought up some feelings I didn't realise I had, I'm just a bit stressed about how it will all go, does that make sense?"

"I think so, but I can't wait to have Mum home, it's going to be great to have her here."

"I know it is. It's me, Tom, it's hard to explain, but it will be fine I'm sure. It's just hard on me, that's all. I've been feeling really strange about it lately."

What else could I tell Tom without actually revealing the truth? How could I tell him that Mum had tried to kill herself in our house and that I was the one who found her that day. It is just easier to explain to Tom that over the last few days I've been a bit stressed about it all.

"Are you feeling better now, Fran?"

"I am, I will be fine, you'll see."

"Right! Tom, my boy, what's on the box now?"

"Don't know, Dad, shall I look?"

"Yeah, go on. Fran, you and Pip going to join us?"

"Ah, no thanks, Dad, I think I'm going to give Pip a bath with loads of bubbles."

"Yeah, bubbly bath, bubbles."

"Okay, lovely."

I leave Dad and Tom deciding what to watch as I pick up Pip and head up the stairs. I grab a fresh towel and pyjamas from the airing cupboard and start running Pip's bath. She sits on the closed toilet lid and starts to sway her little legs back and forth as I add huge squirts of her favourite green bubble bath to the deepening water.

"More, more."

"I can't, Pip, you'll get lost in there if I add any more bubbles."

I undress Pip and gently pop her into her very own bubble-filled world. She loves it, Pip can't stay still in the bath and instantly kicks her arms and legs out like an Olympic swimmer.

"Yeah, kick, kick, Pip, build those little legs up."

I let Pip thrash away and start to add baby shampoo to her hair. This, she isn't so keen on, but I make sure none of the shampoo suds get near her eyes and comfort her by singing "The wheels on the bus".

"That's it, wash your legs with those bubbles."

"Bubbly, bubbles."

After rinsing and washing off the shampoo I just sit for a few minutes and watch my little sister as she splashes her arms and legs around the bath. *It must be nice to be so carefree, just enjoying the next moment, and having no worries.*

"Come on then, little one, let's get you dry."

"Not yet, bubbly, more bubbles yet."

I let Pip play on, why not? She's loving every moment of it.

***

"Well, that was a crap programme, wasn't it?"

"Ha-ha, yeah it was, Dad, I thought it sounded good though, you know with that man trying to find that massive snake. What was it called? An anaconda?"

"Yeah, an anaconda, that's right; what did he say, 'A man eater', well they didn't find anything like that in those waters, did they?"

"No, and we only saw one, and that was too small to eat a human, wasn't it?"

"Yeah, not good, won't be watching anything with him in it again. Right, young man, you going to have a bath after Fran and Pip have finished?"

"Oh, Dad, do I have to?"

"Well, yes you do, Tom."

"Oh, okay, fine. Dad? Is Fran okay?"

"Fran, yeah she's doing okay, love, why do you ask?"

"Well, she's not going to school, is she? And spends most of time up in her room."

"Well, Fran's a bit stressed at the moment, Tom, that's all, but she seems a bit more like her old self tonight, don't you think?"

"I guess so. Stressed, stressed about what? Mum?"

"Yeah, your mum that's right. Look, Fran's a bit older then you and I think she just feels more stressed out about how Mum will cope with her first visit home, especially after being away for such a long time. Do you understand Tom?"

"Yeah, I guess, but I can't wait to have Mum home, even if it is only for a couple of hours at first."

"Well, that's great to hear, Tom. She can't wait to see you all either, and don't worry about your sister, love, Dad will sort it all out okay."

"Okay, all right Dad, I can't wait until Saturday now."

"I know, me either, we'll have a nice few hours together won't we? It's going to be great."

***

"Dad! Dad!… Dad, come quick. It's all right, Pip, I'm okay, I just need to… sit down."

"What is it! Fran, Fran what is it? I'm coming, I'm coming."

"Don't cry, little Pip, I just need to sit down; Dad's coming… da…"

"Jesus, Fran, what's happened? Fran, wake up, Fran. Oh shit, Fran, wake up. Tom, get up here!"

"Coming. What's happening, Dad?"

"Fran, come on love, come on, wake up, wake up."

"What's happened, Dad?"

"It's your sister, she's fainted I think. Quickly Tom, take Pip into her room out of the way."

"What, why, can't I help?"

"No! For God's sake, Tom, take your little sister into her room! Now, please!"

"Oh, come on love, that's it, that's it, just breathe... slowly breathe, that's it, that's it, you're okay."

"Da...d, what, what's happening?"

"You're okay, just breathe, love."

"Pip! Where's Pip?"

"She's fine; Pip's with Tom in her room."

"Oh, Dad, what happened?"

"You must have passed out, love, fainted I guess."

"Ah... God, no. Sit me up, Dad, please sit me up."

"Okay, slowly though, that's it, rest your head against the bath."

"Oh, Dad, it's happening again, I... I felt weird, and hot and sweaty. Oh no, not again, I felt okay earlier, having pizza and playing with Pip. What's happening to me, Dad, am I going crazy?"

"Oh, Fran, of course you're not going crazy, you haven't eaten properly for days, it could be that, couldn't it? Maybe that mixed with your anxiety has made you feel faint. Did it feel like a panic attack do you think?"

"I don't know." *How would I know?* "This felt so different than before, I... I really thought I was dying this time, everything went black. I'm losing it, Dad! I can't go through this again, not again."

"Fucking hell… we've got to get this sorted out, love, shall I call for a doctor?"

"No! Don't do that, I'm seeing Doctor Coakley tomorrow anyway."

"I know but if… if you're fainting, I mean that's a worry, isn't it?"

"Don't call, Dad, please don't call, I'll be okay, I just need to rest again. I haven't eaten much, like you said, so maybe that's got something to do with it."

"Well, maybe, yes, that could be the reason, but just stay sitting for a while now, Fran. Can I get you some water or a squash?"

"Water would be good."

"Tom! Pip! It's all right, I'm all right, I must have passed out or something, I'll be okay again in a minute."

"All right, Fran, Pip's okay as well, we're just playing with her teddies."

"Okay, you can come in the bathroom if you want. Come on, Pip, come see your sister. Tom, bring Pip in, it's okay."

"Okay, coming."

I feel stupid just sitting here alone, that was weird, everything just went black.

"Blimey, Fran, you gave us a scare, you all right?"

"Better, a bit better, sorry. Oh, Pip, it's okay, I'm all better now."

"Here's some water, love, just sip at it. Well, Christ, Fran, that got us all moving, didn't it? I've never seen your brother move so fast!"

I let out a little chuckle after my first sip of water and give Pip a big cuddle. *Shit, that must have scared her.*

"Just stay sitting, Fran, drink some more water and take your time, all right?"

I don't know if I actually fainted, I had the same feelings as earlier, in my maths lesson, but this time I can remember hearing and feeling everything. At school all I can remember is being carried out of the class, I don't recall what happened before that.

"That's it, love, you got some colour coming back now."

"I feel a bit better, Dad, I want to stand up, maybe have a bath in a minute."

"Okay, if you're sure. Let's get you up then, but slowly, okay?"

I push myself up with Dad's help and once on my feet I feel slightly off balance, but my head is starting to feel clearer.

"Just get steady on your feet, Fran, that's it, my love; how do you feel?"

"Yeah, much better thanks, I think I'll take a bath and try to get an early night. I want to get ready for my appointment tomorrow, and I feel really tired all of a sudden."

"Well, I bet you do. Okay, don't have the water too hot though, and bloody shout if you need me, I mean it, Fran, just shout."

"Come on, kids, let's leave Fran to it."

"You sure you're going to be okay, Fran?"

"Oh, thanks, Tom. Yeah, I'll be fine. I'll have a nice relaxing bath and get an early night."

Christ that was scary, what's happening to me? I thought I was dying, it felt like I was falling, falling off a cliff into a dark, cold, empty place. My thoughts as I was falling turned to Pip; she was watching me from a far-off place as I slipped away.

I run my bath, and start to undress, I feel a bit shaky on my feet still as I look in the bathroom mirror. I get into the running bath, it's only a few inches deep but the hot water still feels nice as it almost scalds my skin. I decide my legs need a shave, they feel rough to touch, and I notice some dark flecks of hair as I move my legs side to side in the shallow bath water. As I slowly run the blade over my shins, I misjudge my own pressure on the handle and nick myself twice, once as I put too much weight on the razor, and then again as I quickly try and remove it. *Ouch, shit, that stung.*

As I watch the thin, vein-like spill of blood trickle slowly down my shin and onto my ankle before it tints the hot water pink and then disappears completely into my soapy bath water, I feel a sense of relief and pleasure. The second nick, which is much smaller than the first, release's a much slower trickle of blood. Engrossed by its slow relentless movement, I watch the thin stream of blood run down my calf and slowly drip into the bath water.

I pick up my razor from the edge of the bath and press it hard against my shin, just above the smaller nick, the sharp blade makes me flinch at first, but as I watch the bright red blood spill out again I take in a deep satisfying sigh and feel a sense of relief throughout the whole of my body.

This time, the razor blade has left two thin parallel lines close to each other. This looks like more of a cut then a nick, and the blood is constantly flowing from both this time. I watch again, fascinated as the blood enters my bath water off my ankle and turns the water near to my feet a much darker pink, more like a crimson or burgundy red.

After a while I wash off the slowing trail of blood with my flannel, and just lay myself back into the water. As soon as my legs are submerged, I feel a slight sting on my broken skin, the sting doesn't last long, and I examine the cuts with my finger and notice that the bleeding has come to a complete stop.

What the hell am I doing? Why does that feel so good? Shall I do it again? No one will ever know, will they?

I don't do it again at first, I just continue to wash myself and then apply some shampoo to my hair.

I could do it again, by cutting myself it somehow released a pressure inside of me. I enjoyed seeing my own blood, and it didn't really hurt that much. I could use my other leg next time.

"Fran, you okay in there? You've been in there for ages, love."

"Fine Dad, just enjoying my soak."

"Okay, just checking, come down and say good night if you are having an early night, I'm going to be putting Pip to bed soon."

"Will do."

I don't want to get out yet, the water is becoming cooler though, so I turn on the hot tap, and grab my razor again. This time I try scraping the twin blades down the shin of my other leg. *Fuck, that hurt.* The blades seemed to stick and then jump painfully down my tight skin, the blood this time doesn't seem to be coming at all, instead I just notice that the cut has left a number of small open wounds which look fleshy and white. But after about ten seconds, I start to see the first deep red spots of blood appearing. I take a hold of my calf and with my other hand start to push hard around my fresh razor cuts. After a few seconds the blood begins to piss out of them and spill out in every direction down my shin and calf. For a split second I panic and think, *I've cut too deep, what if I can't stop the bleeding, what if Pip walked in and saw all this blood?*

The sight of all my blood and the strange feeling of pleasure I am experiencing enable me, surprisingly, to switch off all my panicky thoughts, and instead I just begin to focus quite happily on watching my blood as it streams quicker than ever down my lower leg and drip continuously into my bathwater, which has now almost all turned a washed out, kind of pink colour.

I am mental! I am mentally ill. But strangely and perversely this seems to be helping. When I cut myself and watch the flow of blood that produces, I feel in control. I can control my anxiety and thoughts in that moment of pain and blood.

I quickly wash my hair and pull the plug. And as I start to dry myself, I watch as the soapy pinkish water slowly drains away. I enjoyed my bath, I really enjoyed it, not for its soothing hot water and relaxing bubbles, but because I have found, I think, a way to gain some control.

***

"Hi love, nice bath, feeling better?"

"Oh, it was lovely Dad, just what I needed, I feel so much better now."

"Great, I was just going to take Pip up to bed."

"No, no it's fine, let me."

"Are you sure, I don't mind."

"No, honestly, Dad, it's fine."

"Shall I read you a story, Pip?"

"Yeah… story, story. 'The Little Princess'."

"Okay, okay if that's what you want."

"Princess… story, yeah."

"Right, come on then little one, night, all, see you in the morning."

"Okay, night, Fran."

"Fran, before you go up, listen, I'm off tomorrow as you know so we can go to the doctor's together so don't worry about getting up to sort Tom and Pip out in the morning, okay? I'll do it."

"Oh, thanks, Dad, that's great."

"Also, I've asked Pam to come over about nine o'clock so she can watch Pip for me while I pop to the Spar to get some things I need. So, no mad rush in the morning either, okay?"

"Oh, great, sounds good, night, all."

"Sleep well, both, give us a kiss then, my little orange pip."

"Oh, that was a big one! See you in the morning, sweetheart."

***

I only read two to three pages of Pip's book before she is turning over and saying goodnight. I leave her little bedside light on and quietly pull her squeaking door to nearly three quarters shut.

I feel tired, but I also feel in control for the first time since last Saturday evening. I lay out on the top of my duvet and pull up my pyjama bottoms to take a look at my cuts. There are a few wet bloody scab's forming on the deeper cuts, but the little nicks on my other leg look no more than a couple of small drying spots that you might naturally get from time to time.

I close my eyes and try to force myself to remember clearly how I had felt a little earlier in the bath. I spread out my legs and rest my arms down next to me as I start to recall the pleasure I had felt from the pain I had caused myself. Strangely my cuts instantly start to sting as I continue to think about the sense of control I had felt. I push the back of my head deeper into my pillows and, with a sense of satisfaction and contentment throughout my body and mind, I start to close my eyes, which begin to feel heavy while my body begins to feel light.

Chapter 8

God, they're making so much noise. I come around to the sounds of loud talking and laughing from downstairs. I glance at my phone and see its only quarter to eight. Why are they being so noisy? *They never seem to be that loud when I get them up and make breakfast.*

I think about hiding back under my duvet and trying to get some more sleep, but I feel wide awake now and begin thinking about my day ahead. I pick up my phone and start looking at my Facebook and Instagram updates. There are loads, so I only concentrate on the last day's comments and pictures. As I scroll through I feel a sudden panic when I see my name on Tanya's timeline, but thankfully it's just a comment about swimming practice, and nothing about Saturday, or me nearly passing out on Wednesday.

I take a look at my legs and can see that all my cuts have dry scabs on them now. I rub them, and the two smaller scabs on my right leg flake off revealing a new pink layer of skin underneath.

I can still hear the loud noises coming from downstairs as I make my way to the bathroom. Oh,

I wish I could have slept for longer. Now I've got to face the day and think about how I'm feeling inside.

I take my time brushing my teeth but as soon as I look up into the mirror all I can think about suddenly is Mum, Mum is coming home tomorrow. *Oh, no, it's going to be so hard, I can't do it.* I will myself not to start feeling anxious again but as soon as that thought has entered my mind, I begin to feel the familiar tingle start in my arms. I swill my mouth out and wipe my face as the tingle now reaches my toes. *Keep busy, Fran, take a bath, just keep busy.* I will take a bath, but not right now.

Last night, before bed, I had pictured myself getting ready for today. I would sleep until about nine, by then Tom would have gone to school and Dad would be busy with Pip downstairs. I would read any updates or messages on my phone and then run myself a nice deep bath. I would use my razor again and see if it helps ease my worries and gives me comfort. But now, all I feel is anxious, anxious because of Mum, because I've got hours to kill before my appointment, anxious about being downstairs for ages with Dad and Pip. I sit on the toilet and start to feel my chest; my heart is now beating so fast that I can see my pyjama top moving. As I remove my hand and look down, I can see that my legs have started to shake, That's new.

"You in the toilet, love?"

"Yes… hi, Dad, won't be a minute."

"Okay, just need a pee, that's all."

"Okay, nearly finished."

"I'll pop back up in second."

"Won't be long."

I flush the loo, and straight away feel rushed. *I hate being rushed!*

"Toilet's free!"

"Lovely, on my way, thanks, Fran."

I head back into my bedroom; *This morning is not going to plan at all. I've got too much time to think now.* Feeling flustered, and clammy all over, I concentrate on sorting my clothes out for the day. I pick out some dark blue leggings and a black t-shirt; the sun is out again, and I know I'm going to sweat so the thin cotton T-shirt, leggings and my trainers will be fine.

"Can I come in, Fran?"

"Yes."

"Morning, love, I didn't expect to see until later; Tom and Pip are all sorted, and I've just finished cleaning the kitchen. How you feeling?"

"Nervous, really nervous to be honest, Dad."

"What, about the doctor's?"

"Well sort of… I mean I think that's going to be okay, but I'm more nervous about Mum."

"Oh, I know it's going to feel strange having your mum home for a few hours, but we've got to give it a try, haven't we?"

"I know. But you haven't even told her about me, have you, Dad?"

"I've spoken to her three times this week, but no I haven't told her about last Saturday or you seeing the doctor, no I didn't mention that."

"Oh… well, I thought Mum should know, 'she needs to know,' that's what you said."

"I know what I said, Fran, but… if I had told her, I think it would really set her back."

"Oh." *That's fantastic Dad, thanks, that really makes me feel better!*

"I'm sorry, love, but for now I think it's for the best."

"All right, all right, fine."

"Let's see what the doctor says, we could talk it through with her if you like?"

"Maybe, but Dad… I think I would like to talk to Dr Coakley by myself."

"What? I've taken the day off, love."

"I know, and I appreciate that, what I meant was, if we both see her at first, I wouldn't mind speaking with her for a bit on my own."

"I see, okay, if that's what you want, no problem. It will get sorted, Fran, you'll see. Right, I'm going to make sure Tom is ready for school and Pip is okay, so see you downstairs in a bit, okay?"

"Ok." Dad doesn't understand me, not one little bit. I'm all alone, no one cares about what I say or how having Mum come back to our house makes me feel.

I feel angry again, annoyed with everything. I shove my clothes off my bed and chuck my phone to the floor. I'm not going to be able to get through this, I can't pretend everything is okay, not to my mum, she'll know something is very wrong, I can't do this.

***

I pick up my clothes I'd thrown earlier off the floor and try to fold them neatly but can't, so I chuck them back onto my bed in a heap; as I do my phone makes a sound. I look at it and can see that it's getting low on battery, so I plug it in to charge. As I bend down the morning sun strikes my face. I glance out of my window and notice that the low sun is now behind a small fluffy white cloud. It's hidden glare still feels hot on my face though as I continue watching as the cloud slowly drifts away. The sun without its cloud cover now looks an intense orange colour; it makes me squint as the brightness streams through my window and burns its warmth onto my bedroom floor.

I hear our front door opening and look down from my bedroom window, I can see Tom as he heads off down the street. I notice that his head is hung low as he strides forward. *Can he see where he is going?* I think to myself. *I wonder what he's thinking about?* A surge of guilt hits me. *I should make more time for him. Shit, I hope he never has to feel like I do.*

I head to the bathroom and start running my bath. The sudden rush I get when I think about using my razor again is unexplainable. I enjoy a bath, who doesn't? Hot, soapy water and time to relax and think. But the anticipation of having a bath seems different for me now. *Could I feel the same pleasure and release as before?* I decided when I first cut myself yesterday that this thing, this accidental feeling is going to be all mine, the self-inflicted pain, which is so strangely enjoyable and relieving, is all I can think about now. The anticipation of its intense pleasure feels overwhelming.

Excitedly, I add some bubble bath and start getting undressed, the anticipation now sends adrenalin surging through my body, and for a brief moment my anxieties have completely disappeared. I check to make sure the bathroom door is locked and as I start to turn the metal lock I hear my dad's familiar voice coming from downstairs.

***

"What shall we watch, my little orange Pip?"

"Tubbies! Tubbies, please, Dad."

"*Teletubbies*, are you sure? Haven't you got bored of them yet?"

"Yeah, *Teletubbies*, please."

"Okay, if that's what you want, my darling. Let's pop that in for you, and then you come and sit on Daddy's lap, yeah?"

"Yeah, Daddy's lap."

***

I make my first cut with the twin blade razor just above the first two smaller marks which are just still visible on the middle of my right shin. As soon as I feel the stinging pain, I relax. I watch my blood trickle out from both thin cuts and notice that its flow is following on a different path from yesterday. Instead of flowing down my shin towards my ankle, the blood, which looks thicker somehow, is now heading to the side and around my calf. *I guess my body position is slightly different from yesterday, or maybe I've cut deeper than before.*

Again, I watch with fascination as the blood finally enters the water; I feel aroused somehow, my stomach feels warm and I have a glow all over my body. I cut again, wanting, needing that feeling to persist. After the second cut, which is definitely deeper than my first, I just lay myself back, putting my head under the bath water. *Silence, oh how nice to have silence.*

Whilst my head is submerged all I can hear is my own heartbeat and the distant watery echo of moving water. I close my eyes and drift off deep into my innermost thoughts. *How have I ended up here? I can't keep doing this, how can I swim with cuts all over me? Do I want to swim anymore? If cutting myself helps, that makes me mentally ill, doesn't it?* I lift my confused head out the water, shaking it as I do so. I've lost any sense of time, but my water is getting cooler, so I start adding some more hot water. I must have just been lying here, deep in my own thoughts, enjoying the near perfect silence for quite a while now.

After feeling the fresh hot water's effect on my skin, I decide to cut the other leg. Again, I push hard on the handle of the razor as it releases its perverse pain. The stinging sensation is more prolonged this time, *I must have really pushed hard. God, why does this feel so good?*

***

Knock, knock.

"Come in, Pam, it's open."

"Morning, both, oh, what a lovely sunny one again."

"I know, fantastic, isn't it?"

"Really warm already. How's it all going? Fran up and about?"

"Yeah, I said she could sleep in a bit, but she was still up early, I think she's in the bath now."

"Oh, well I guess she's a bit nervous about the doctor's today, I know I'm up really early when I've got an appointment to go to. Hello, Pip, you all right, little darling?"

"Tubbies on."

"Oh, lovely darling, that's good."

"Yeah, *Teletubbies* again! Anyway, it's been a bit of a night for Fran."

"Why, what's happened now?"

"Well, Fran was giving Pip a bath and I heard her shouting for me, so I ran upstairs, and Fran was on the bathroom floor, it looked like she had passed out."

"Oh, no!"

"Yeah, Pip was fine, luckily she was out of the bath, Fran must have been drying her I guess, and then, well fainted."

"Christ, Frankie, what did you do?"

"I just talked to her, you know tried to make her come around, I could see she was breathing, and there was plenty of colour in her cheeks. So... I don't know, maybe after about thirty seconds I guess, she started to come around, her eyes opened, and she started talking."

"I bet you were really worried? God, Frankie, what happened then?"

"Well, I was… I was really worried at first, then I sat her up against the bath and gave her some water, she soon came around, thank God, and poor old Tom and Pip didn't know what was going on."

"I bet; they okay though?"

"Yeah, they're fine, Tom was a big help actually, he kept an eye on his little sister while I was with Fran in the bathroom."

"God, Frankie, it doesn't rain – it bloody pours for you at the moment, doesn't it?"

"Oh, I know Pam, it's been a tough week. With all that going on Saturday, and then Fran freaking out on Monday, yeah, you could say it's been a strange old couple of days. I just want Fran to get through today, you know what I mean? Hopefully the doctor will suggest something, I don't know, maybe get Fran to talk to someone, a counsellor or something."

"What a week, ah? Yeah, that's a good idea I think, Frankie, maybe the doctor will suggest that. Fran would find that helpful I'm sure, don't you? She hasn't ever really talked about her mum, not about the suicide attempt or her finding Launa, has she?"

"Not really, no. And yes, I think talking to someone can only help. I've tried to get her to open up, but no, she's kept a lot locked away I think, Pam."

"I know, love, it must be so hard on her, well, on all of you, but you know what I mean, Fran finding Launa like that. God, it sends shudders down my spine."

"I know, I can't imagine how it made Fran feel, Horrible thought, isn't it? Fran did mention that yesterday, you know, about finding Launa, and now how she feels weird about seeing her mum back at home."

"What did she say?"

"Not much, just that she feels weird about seeing her mum, you know, back in the house."

"Well that's good, at least she's talked a little about it. It's going to be strange for you all, isn't it, maybe even stranger for Fran, I guess."

"Yeah, it will. God, I hope it goes well, I've spoken to Launa, and she sounds more positive, Pam. I think it's the right thing to do, we've got to move forward, haven't we? I want her home, you know that, Pam, I want and need Launa back home where she belongs."

"I know, Frankie, and it's happening, she is getting better, and it can only help her, spending some time in her home, surrounded by her family."

"Exactly, that's true, that's what I think, things will work out."

"They will, Frankie, they will. So, what time's Fran's appointment again today?"

"Not until eleven thirty, so I'll pop to the shop in a minute and grab a quick shower before we go later."

"Okay, you've got plenty of time then, Frankie, and I'm here now as well to look after this little one."

"Great, thanks, Pam, and like I said, let's hope the doctor comes up with some ideas for Fran, and then we can just all look forward to having Launa, for a few hours tomorrow."

***

The water's turning cold again, so I decide it must be time to get out. I would rather just lay here though and carry on enjoying my strange intense emotional release I seem to be getting from causing my own pain and seeing my blood.

I give myself a quick wash all over with soap and pull the plug, I notice that my new cuts have now stopped bleeding, so I wash off the sticky bloody remains with my flannel. *It must be after nine by now, but I haven't heard Aunty Pam downstairs.*

Out of my bath now, I spend some time applying my moisturiser, taking special care not to rub too hard over my fresh, thin razor cuts, which still sting but have stopped giving me that intense pleasure. Drying my hair, I take a look in the mirror. At first the steam has made it only possible to see the bottom few inches of the mirror, so I wipe the rest of it off with my towel. My face looks pink from the hot bath water. I continue to look at my face and start drying my hair. Suddenly I get that horrible, now familiar, frightened feeling as it hits hard inside my guts.

If only I could stay in my bath forever, then I wouldn't have to feel like this ever again.

Back in my room now, I roll on some deodorant and start my make-up. I wonder what the doctor's going to ask me today. I run through a scenario of how I expect things to go. *How have you been, Fran? Have you been feeling anxious? Have you returned to school? Have you read the booklet I gave you? If so, have you tried the relaxation techniques? Have you talked about your mum with anybody?*

Whatever happens at the doctor's, I know I won't be mentioning my bathtime. Dad, I'm sure, will tell the doctor about me passing out, and that I've not really being eating that much. He'll avoid talking about Mum. I know now that he can't see and feel what I feel, he just can't see beyond Mum's slow return home, and her then coming home permanently.

***

Make up almost done. *God, it's not even nine thirty yet.* I finish my make-up by applying some flesh colour lipstick and concealer. *Shit, it's ages yet until we've got to go to the doctor's.*

Wanting time to pass quickly only ever makes it seem to go slower. So, I begin getting dressed and think about reading some of my booklet that the doctor gave me. *That will kill some time, just concentrate on the booklet.* I haven't had breakfast yet but don't feel hungry at all, my stomach has been so upset over the last week that I just can't think about food; *I can make a cuppa and maybe grab a biscuit just before me and Dad leave.*

Reading through the first few pages, I come to the part about how a thought can trigger a physical response. Those words really strike true with me, I didn't realise just how powerful a thought could be. I've noticed in myself that as soon as I have a negative thought it starts to cause some sort of physical response, like my heart beating faster or having those horrible pins and needles in my arms, then legs. I read some more but start getting frustrated when I can't find the part which explains how to stop your negative thoughts in the first place. I'm starting to understand more about anxiety, but doubt this booklet has any real answer on what I'm really experiencing.

I know what seems to stop my negative thoughts, but I can't do that forever, can I? What about my swimming? I can't swim with cuts all over me. Everyone will notice. People will point and laugh. Maybe I don't want to swim any more anyway.

It's nearly ten o'clock by the time I finish looking at my booklet. I found the part on controlled breathing techniques again but didn't bother trying any.

I hear Pip's unmistakable cry from downstairs and then notice Aunty Pam's voice as she tries to console Pip. I didn't hear Aunty Pam arrive which is strange because she tends to make a bit of an entrance. I check the time on my phone again to make sure I'm not going completely mad and see that it's just past ten o'clock. I thought Aunty Pam was getting here for nine o'clock. So, still feeling confused, I wonder where my head must have been for the last hour or so. I can't hear my dad's voice over Pip's crying but guess that he's popped out, maybe down to the Spar or Porky's, our butcher's.

I take a few deep breaths and try to ready myself for facing Aunty Pam and all her queries. I take one last look at myself in my mirror and check my make-up and hair before leaving my sanctuary and heading downstairs.

"Who's this coming, Pip? Is it your big sister do you think?"

"Yeah, Franny, Franny home."

"Hi, both."

"Morning, love, nice sunny one again, isn't it?"

"I know, really nice morning, it's so warm already. Hello, my little Pip, what you watching, then?"

"*Smurfs*, Franny, it's *Smurfs* film."

"Oh, that's good then, they're funny looking, aren't they? Come and give me a big cuddle, Pip."

"Yeah, big cuddle, big cuddle."

"Oh… that's a nice one, that's a big one, love, that makes Fran feel better; give me a kiss."

Pip gives me a big wet kiss right on my lips, it feels so good. I start to swing Pip from side to side and she lets out an excited scream as I raise her up above my head and blow hard into her chubby belly.

"God, you're getting heavy, I don't know if I can hold on." Again, Pip screams out. I pretend to drop her this time, and again she happily screams out."

"Up you go! Down you go!" Pip is in fits of laughter now and I can't help but smile at her.

"Whoa, hold on, Pip. She loves that, Fran, bless her."

"Up again! Again!"

"Just once more then, okay?"

"Oh."

I lift Pip up as high as I can go, then dramatically drop her before catching her again and putting her back down onto the front room floor.

"Can I make you a cuppa, Fran?"

"No, it's okay thanks, Aunty Pam; God, I'm knackered now, Pip's getting heavy. I'll make a cuppa in a minute, thanks."

"Okay, how you feeling, love?"

"Ah… a bit nervous, I guess."

"Oh, love, you're bound to be a bit nervous, you've had a tough week too, let's just see what the doctor has to say about it later."

"Yeah, I guess so, I don't know, it's… hard to explain, Aunty Pam, I just don't feel right."

"I know, love, it's so hard for you, so hard for all of you. But you've got lots of support, love, I mean I'm here if you ever just want to talk."

"I know, I know that, thanks, Aunty Pam."

I appreciate Aunty Pam saying that, but really don't think I can talk to her about any of this scary and distressing stuff that I'm experiencing. I head for the kitchen and rifle through the biscuit barrel, the only ones left are some sad looking custard creams which are mainly broken in half, so I just take one of the broken halves and decide to put the kettle on. As I do that I hear the front door opening.

"Hey, you, oh you look nice, love."

"Yeah, yeah, very funny, Dad."

"No, I mean it, you look…well you look good, that's all."

"Well thanks, Dad, but it's just some leggings and a T-shirt, so don't get to carried away."

"Ha-ha. Fair enough, look I got us all a breakfast roll from Porky's."

"Oh nice, I'm not that hungry though, Dad, to be honest."

"Well, just eat what you can, I'm sure I'll manage what's left."

"Thanks, Dad."

"Yeah, thanks Frankie, that's a real treat; lovely."

"My pleasure. Fran, grab a few plates out, then."

"Will do."

"Pip, I thought you could share some of mine, you love your sausages, don't you?"

"Sasasge, sasasge and ketchup."

"That's right, ketchup all over them, ha-ha."

I put our plates out and end up making a cuppa for everyone anyway. I manage to eat more than I thought my increasingly worried-feeling stomach would allow.

"Enjoyed that, Fran?"

"Yeah, thanks, Dad, I ate more than I thought I would."

"Good stuff, I'll tidy up if you want to play with Pip or something."

"What time is it, Dad?"

"Ah, just before twenty to eleven."

"Okay, I thought I might just read a bit more of that booklet, you know, the one Dr Coakley gave me."

"Oh yeah, good idea. Shall we walk down or drive to the doctor's, do you think?"

"Um… walk I think, Dad, it's so nice out there today."

"True, okay, we'll walk then. Say, leave at about ten past eleven, something like that?"

"Yeah, sounds good, thanks for breakfast, Dad, I really enjoyed that."

***

I leave Dad and Aunty Pam tidying up downstairs and head straight for the bathroom. Over our breakfast rolls I suddenly felt so strange again, not faint or sweaty like before, but like I wasn't really there, like I was looking at myself from across the room, but no one could see or hear me. I could hear Dad, Aunty Pam and even Pip talking and laughing, but I wasn't involved in any of it, I was invisible to them all.

I've only got twenty minutes, I can't have a bath and use my razor in that time, what can I do?

I just stare at myself in the bathroom mirror, I could just pull my leggings down and make a cut that way.

I shake my head, as to say no to myself, but the thought of relieving my tension is the only thing driving my thoughts now. So, I pull my leggings down and sit on the toilet, pulling the lid down first. My razor sits in one of those plastic cups you use for your toothbrush and toothpaste. So, I grab my razor whilst sitting down. My legs look sore but don't really feel that way. I take a big sigh, close my eyes and push the razor deep into the top of my shin of my left leg. I scream a little but manage to control my volume by biting down hard onto my top lip. The almost instant gratification is overwhelming, I feel my whole body loosen like a piece of stretched elastic when it's cut and starts to unravel. I haven't got time to watch the flow of my blood this time so instead push the razor onto my skin again. I take a deep breath out as the pain first hits me, then I take a long breath in as the overwhelming feeling of joy and intensity heightens, it feels more powerful and satisfying than before.

I spend the next few minutes dapping toilet paper onto my cuts, it soaks it up really quickly, and after only using a few pieces I see that the blood is slowing, and it only reappears in a tiny amount on each cut. *It will soon dry, no one will ever know, I don't need to always be in the bath to feel that pain. I can do this anywhere.*

***

"Fran, it's nearly time to go if we're walking."

"Okay, Dad, one minute."

I quickly check my legs again by fully pulling down my leggings as I sit on my bed. They look fine, the blood has definitely stopped. I stand up and I take a quick glance in my mirror, I tidy up my hair then grab for my mobile which is still on charge, and I'm ready, *ready as I'll ever be.*

"Ready, Dad."

"Okay… see you in a bit, Pam; see you soon, little Pip."

"Yeah, hope it goes well, say bye, bye, Pip."

"Bye, bye."

"Oh… thanks, Pip, see you soon, Aunty Pam."

"Okay, love, you'll be fine, I'm sure."

Dad opens the front door and we head off. As soon I reach the pavement I can feel the heat of the sun as it burns the back of my head and neck. We walk side by side and Dad is puffing away on his roll-up and straightening his sunglasses as he walks.

"Didn't you bring your sunglasses, love?"

"Oh, no, I forgot them; can I go back and get them?"

"Well, run, then, we don't want to be late, do we?"

I quickly sprint up our street, enjoying the feeling of the breeze as I push myself to go faster. I get to our house and push open the door.

"Ah... you all right, Fran, what's happened?"

"No, nothing, just forgot my sunglasses."

"Oh, okay, yeah, you definitely need them today."

I rush up the stairs and find my glasses sitting amongst all my make-up which is on top of my chest of drawers. I hesitate for a second, and suddenly feel really, really scared, almost like in that split second I've seen something so horrific and devastating that I don't know how to react to it. *The weirdest feeling ever.* I physically try and shake that awful feeling off by shaking my head and then my arms, it seems to work, aware of the time I rush down the stairs two steps at a time."

"Got them, see you in a bit, bye."

"Okay, bye, Fran."

By the time I get to Dad, he's rolling another fag whilst sitting on a brick wall outside a house on Pine Rise.

"Come on, love, we're going have to get going."

"I know, sorry, Dad, I couldn't find them at first."

"No worries, it's less than ten minutes or so away, so we should be fine."

We reach Fore Street and decide to cross opposite the Fountain Inn. The doctor's is situated just down from the leisure centre in a cul-de-sac. It's a fairly new looking building, with small flower beds and some hanging baskets at the front of it. To the side of it is a small red brick building which is where the local pharmacy is.

"Nearly there, love, you doing okay?"

"Oh, Dad, I don't know, I don't know what to expect, I mean what do you think she'll want to talk about?"

"Well, a bit more about how you felt on the Monday, and how your week's been, I guess."

"Oh, yeah, I suppose so. Do you think the doctor may give me something, a pill or whatever to make me feel better?"

"Well maybe, love, I don't know. Let's see what she says, you never know the doctor may suggest that you talk to someone, you know about how you're feeling and that, instead of just giving you some medication."

"What a psychiatrist, you mean?"

"Well, maybe not a psychiatrist then, but a counsellor, someone like that, someone who you can really talk to. Do you think that would help, Fran? I mean is that something you would be willing to do, do you think?

"I think so, yes I would, Dad. But I still can't really explain in words how I feel, so how will that work?"

"I'm not really sure, but these counsellors are really good at getting people to talk you know. So, if the doctor thinks seeing a counsellor is a good idea, I think you should give it a go, love."

"Okay, I guess so, let's wait and hear what the doctor thinks, then."

"Okay, that makes sense, come on then, we're almost there, what time you got, Fran?"

"It's… twenty-three minutes past."

"Brilliant, good timing, that. Fran, stop a minute, look… I think we should tell the doctor about you passing out last night, don't you?"

"Oh, Dad, no! Honestly, that was because I hadn't eaten, that's all."

"Well, I'm not so sure, love, I mean, it could have been that, but why not tell the doctor? She might be able to explain why it happened."

"I don't want to, Dad! No, I don't want to!

Dad doesn't reply to me but just shakes his head as we start to make our way through the doors and into the reception. As we enter, I instantly recognise the receptionist from Monday, she looks flustered and I notice that the reception has a long queue. I can see, as I look through to the waiting room, that it's jam-packed full of people, too. My heart jumps into my mouth and already I start to feel ill and panicky as I think about sitting amongst all those people.

"Morning; Franny Goode to see Doctor Coakley for eleven thirty please."

"Okay, thanks… let's have a look… fine, yes, please just take a seat in the waiting room through there and Doctor Coakley will be with you as soon as possible."

"Wow, you're really busy today!"

"Very, very busy, but you'll be pleased to hear that Franny is next to be seen, so it shouldn't be too long for you, Mr Goode."

"Great, that's good to hear, thanks."

"Yeah, thanks," I say.

"See, love, we won't have to wait too long, let's try and find a seat."

"Okay."

There are no free seats, so me and Dad lean against a wall which is opposite a small kiddie play area and a table with various magazines and books on it. I try to just focus on looking down, down at my trainers and then the grey worn out looking carpet which covers the waiting room floor, but as I do, I start to feel dizzy and sick, so I look up, and without really looking at anything in particular, start to feel that everybody is staring at me.

"You okay, Fran?

"Feel a bit dizzy, Dad."

"Here, hold onto my arm."

I lean into Dad and then hold firmly onto Dad's right arm; as I do, I begin to well up. It takes all of my efforts to hold back my tears. I instinctively reach down and start scratching my right shin, I feel an instant sting as I must have removed one of the drying scabs; I scratch again and can feel a dampness under my leggings.

"Fran, you okay? What you doing, love."

"I'm okay now, I've just got an itch."

I stop scratching, and start to feel slightly better, I let go of Dad's arm and rest my head back against the cold wall behind me, I shut my eyes for a moment.

"Franny Goode, please."

I hear my name being called for me to see Doctor Coakley; she calls again and me and Dad step away from the wall and turn instinctively to the right. As we do, I see Doctor Coakley who is standing outside of the double doors that lead into the corridor and to her room.

"Morning, both."

"Morning, Doctor."

"Morning, Mr Goode; hi, Fran."

"Hi, Doctor."

"Just down here and on the right, just like last time."

"Okay, thanks, Doctor."

Doctor Coakley shows us into her room and gestures for us both to sit down. The room looks different somehow; on Monday it felt smaller and seemed darker. I notice some childlike paintings hanging framed on the wall, also there is a large square window behind her desk which is partly opened allowing the sun to fill the whole room.

"Well, how have things been since I saw you last, Fran."

"Um... well, not great."

"Ah, okay, can you tell me a bit more about that then?"

"Um... I've been feeling really nervous, nervous about everything really."

"I see, can you think of anything in particular that makes you feel more nervous than... say something else, it could be being around lots of people for instance, or standing in a queue?"

"Well, I felt quite panicky when I was queuing with my dad at reception, just a minute ago."

"Okay, so have you been feeling like that, when you're at home, say, with no queue or lots of people around."

"Not always, but most of the time I seem to feel anxious, anxious about something or other, yeah."

"Okay, Fran, that's very helpful. Have you been back to school since I last saw you?"

"Ah... I did manage to go on Wednesday, but felt so ill... I think it was Wednesday evening that I started to feel ill, so I didn't go on Thursday, no."

"Okay, and when you say you felt so ill, was that something other than feeling anxious, like an upset stomach or headache, maybe?"

"Um… well, my stomach was playing up, wasn't it, Dad?"

"It was, it was, yeah. Wednesday, Fran said she felt sick, Doctor. We had some tea, sausages I think, and not long after Fran was saying she felt like she had a stomach-ache."

"Okay, thanks, Mr Goode. How is your stomach now, Fran, any better?"

"Well, I don't feel sick anymore, but when I get anxious my belly is all over the place, it feels like… excitement, but not in a nice way."

"Fine, okay, Fran. Well that makes a lot of sense, remember what we talked about on Monday? The effects that adrenalin has on our bodies?"

"I think so, yeah, you said adrenalin is released when we feel anxious, something like that?"

"That's right. I mentioned the effects of adrenalin as it surges through your body when we feel anxious. Now, feeling anxious about… say, being on an edge of a cliff, it's very natural to feel anxious about that, so, by being anxious and experiencing a surge of adrenalin in that circumstance is completely normal and justified. Where anxiety gets confusing, Fran, is when we have an anxious thought or feeling when there is no obvious threat. Like… say, sitting at home watching TV; if we become anxious in those sorts of circumstance, then the effect, mentally and physically can become very uncomfortable and frightening. Does that make some sense, Fran?"

"I think so. So, am I always going to feel anxious then, even if I don't need to be?"

"No, not at all, there are many things we can try to control our anxiety. Firstly, I think seeing someone in our mental health department would be the best idea. Now, that may sound a bit scary, Fran, but believe me the people over at Okement Mental Health Services are fantastic. They offer one to one counselling, group sessions, cognitive behaviour therapy, which I'll explain more about in a minute; they really do take care of their patients, Fran, they really listen. I couldn't speak more highly of the place."

"Okay, that sounds good, I think that could be helpful, don't you, Dad?"

"Yes, yes, I do, I think that sounds positive and seems to be the best way forward for Fran; but how do we sort all that out, Doctor?"

"You don't, is the short answer. I do. I'll refer Fran to the department and send over any notes I may have and then within a couple of weeks or so a letter will inform you of an assessment appointment. Basically, the assessment appointment is for the department to obviously get to meet you, Fran, discuss any issues you're experiencing, answer any questions you might have about what the department offers, those sorts of things. The assessment meeting last for about forty to fifty minutes and at the end of it the counsellor will suggest the best way to move forward and offer a follow up set of appointments."

"Okay, thanks, Doctor. So, you think it's definitely down to anxiety, then?"

"I believe so, yes, Mr Goode. All the symptoms are there and seeing you again, Fran, and considering your own explanations of how you're feeling, I'm in no doubt that you are struggling to deal with your own anxiety."

"Is there anything I can take, Doctor, just to help stop me feeling like this all the time? I mean, my heartbeat always feels so fast, and then that seems to make my physical problems start."

"Well, yes, there are medications we can prescribe."

"Will they help, I mean can they make me get better, feel normal?"

"They certainly can help, but I find CBT, cognitive behaviour therapy, to be the best first step to regaining control of your own mental health. Let me explain briefly how cognitive behaviour therapy works. Basically, it's what we call a talking therapy, it deals with how we think and behave by explaining how our thoughts, feelings and physical responses are all interconnected. So, the therapy challenges our negative thoughts and teaches us how to break the cycle of anxiety."

"Yeah, that makes a lot of sense, Doctor. I read something about that in that booklet you gave me."

"Great, well I think this should be our first step then, Fran, get you referred and start some cognitive behaviour therapy as soon as we can."

"Okay, thanks, but you said I could be waiting for a least two weeks before I have my assessment appointment, so I won't see anybody for weeks yet. I feel so desperate, Doctor, is there nothing I can have? Just to help me now."

"You're right, it could take couple of weeks for your appointment. But also, Fran, most anxiety medication takes at least two weeks to fully begin to work in your system."

"Oh, I see, but I just want to feel better... now. I can't keep feeling like this. I can't put up with it any longer."

"I do understand, Fran; I know it must feel so difficult for you. Look, what I can do in the short term is prescribe a beta blocker. Now, beta blockers work by decreasing the activity of the heart by blocking the actions of adrenalin. They work almost instantly and are especially effective in the short term, so they can help with your symptoms, like accelerated heartbeat, for example. Does that sound like it could help?"

"Oh, it does, Doctor, thanks, thanks a lot."

"Well, like I say, it's only a short-term solution but if it helps, then I'm happy to prescribe some today."

"Yes, thanks, Doctor."

"Okay, let's do that, then. I'll just print that off for you, and like I said these work almost instantly so take one when you start to feel anxious, preferably with food if you can."

"Okay."

"Thanks, Doctor, I think Fran just needed to know that there was something that could help, you know, help today."

"I understand, and I'm sure, Mr Goode, that this medication will alleviate some of Fran's symptoms."

"Thanks, Doctor, that's a big help. Also, Doctor, I'm not sure if Fran wanted to have a word with you in private; Fran, is that what you said?"

"Yes, if that's okay, Doctor, I would I think."

"Yes, absolutely fine. Okay then, I'll sort out the prescription which you can get next door at the pharmacy, and then I'll refer Fran to the Okement mental health team, okay? Thanks for coming, Mr Goode, it's always important to have family support, and I'm sure Fran is going to be fine. Is there anything else you would like to ask before you go?"

"Um… no, nothing I can think of this minute, thanks again, Doctor. Fran, I'll wait for you out the front, okay?

"Okay, see you in a minute, Dad."

"Bye, Mr Goode."

Now that I'm sitting here on my own, I instantly feel terrified and a bit stupid, I also can't remember what I wanted to say when Dad wasn't going to be in the room.

"Okay, Fran, how can I help?"

"Um… sorry, Doctor, I had planned it all out in my head and now I've gone completely blank?" *How embarrassing, I can feel my cheeks turn red and I want the floor to swallow me up whole.*

"It's okay, take your time, Fran."

"Ah… okay, well, it's about how I'm feeling, the anxiety and all that. I can't get through to my Dad, I mean he doesn't listen to me, you know, really listen to what I'm saying to him."

"Sure, well, that's hard, Fran, but give me an example, what doesn't he really listen to you about?"

"About Mum really, he never listens to me about Mum."

"Okay, and why is that do you think?"

"Oh… that's a hard one. I… guess he's so keen to have Mum home that whatever I say about how that makes me feel, he just ignores it somehow."

"Okay, I understand. Look, Fran, I think talking to one of the counsellors over at Okement is really going to help you with all of this. Like I said, they are brilliant listeners, and I feel that you will gain a lot from just being able to talk to someone who is a professional when it comes to dealing with mental health issues. Once you start your cognitive behaviour therapy, you'll be surprised how quickly things can improve.

"Thanks, Doctor."

"Was that all, Fran?"

"I think so, I just needed to get that of my chest. Dad cares, of course he does, but I needed to have someone to tell that to."

"Of course, Fran, I understand, it's not always easy to be heard, especially when there's lots going on. So, if that's it, just take this prescription next door, and don't hesitate to contact us if you need any more information, or need to talk, okay?"

"Okay, thanks again, Doctor, bye now, bye, Doctor."

"Bye, Fran, take care now."

I retrace my earlier footsteps and head along the corridor towards the waiting room. Once I'm through the still packed waiting room I head past reception and can see Dad through the main doors, he's smoking a roll-up and is standing on the opposite side of the surgery car park.

"All right, love, that went well, don't you think?"

"Yeah, it went well. Shall I go and get my prescription?"

"Yes, just let me finish my smoke and we can go together."

I just want to go get my medication and go home, so Dad's small delay irritates me instantly.

"The doctor made a lot of sense, Fran, and that cognitive therapy sounds really good; don't you think? I know your mum has had that type of therapy at Park Place, and it really helped her."

"Has she? I didn't know that, and yes, it does sound helpful, Dad."

My head is spinning now; any mention of my mum and I can't help but think that I'm somehow destined to completely break down like she did. For now, I can't see beyond just getting my medication and being on my own up in my bedroom.

"Okay, let's go to the pharmacy then, Fran."

"Okay."

We take the short walk to the pharmacy and are faced with another queue, but this time its smaller, and quieter. Dad hands over my prescription and we manage to find a seat in the small waiting area.

"Do you want to do anything after this, Fran?"

"Oh, no, not today, Dad. I feel really tired after having to take all that in."

"Okay, that's fine, yeah, there was a lot to take in, I know, but some positive stuff I thought."

"There was."

I notice the man behind the pharmacy as he picks his way through the boxes which are all packed neatly in white open draws above him. I take a look at my phone and scroll through some updates, but my mind is elsewhere.

When will I get my tablets? Shall I take one straight away? How will it make me feel? God, I'm on medication and I'm going to be in therapy!

My thoughts are interrupted when a woman with a high-pitched voice calls out my name.

"Miss Franny Goode!"

"Oh hi, yeah, that's me."

"Okay, what's your date of birth, please?"

"Eighth of the Tenth, Two Thousand and Four."

"Okay, so you get free prescriptions then, Miss Goode."

"Great, thank you."

"And your address and postcode please, Miss Goode?"

"Twenty-two Oak View, EX4 1PP."

"Lovely, there you go, Miss Goode."

"Thank you."

Me and Dad leave the pharmacy and start walking back home. When we reach the clock tower on Fore Street I suddenly feel dizzy again, my legs seem to be off balance and my vision starts to blur. I'm so eager to get to the safety of home and my bedroom that I just continue to walk next to Dad and don't mention how I feel.

"So, Fran, tomorrow my plan is to go pick up your mum for eleven o'clock."

"Oh, okay."

"Yes, then obviously head back home and well... we'll just see how things go. I thought maybe we could have a little wander after we've all caught up."

"Sounds good."

"So, your aunty is coming over for about ten o'clock tomorrow, okay?"

"Yeah."

"Look, Fran, I know it's going to feel strange having Mum home, but it's going to be strange for all of us. We've got to try, haven't we?"

"Yeah, I know Dad, I know."

***

By the time we get home I feel seriously tired and emotional. I quickly say hi to Pip and Aunty Pam, make a pint of squash and head upstairs. Dad hasn't said a word after explaining about picking Mum up tomorrow, so I leave him sitting in the front room making his roll-up.

I collapse onto my bed, burying my face into my pillows and begin crying, uncontrollably crying.

Why me? I can't think straight; I can't carry on.

I tear open the small rectangular paper bag with my medication in and quickly try to read the first set of instructions I see that it mentions taking the tablets with food and not to exceed the recommended daily dosage I can't think about food so just place one of the small white circular tablets on my tongue and wash it down with a big gulp of orange squash.

I consider running myself a bath, but feeling as useless and lethargic as I do, after being at the doctor's and being told I needed therapy, I decide to close my curtains to block out the sun and then just get under my covers instead. I pull my duvet all the way over my head, and hope, just hope that I can sleep.

Please work, please let these tablets help me, please let me sleep and wake up feeling normal again.

***

I come around to the sound of Tom's voice, it sounds like he's out the front with Dad. Tom's shouting out loud, so I guess they're playing football. Tom is laughing with Dad, I guess he's excited because school's finished for another week, and he's probably even more excited that it's treat night and that he can stuff himself with a big fish supper from Fat Eddie's, soon.

It must be well after three then if Tom's home. God, I've managed to sleep a good few hours.

I become aware that my mouth is dry, so I reach for my squash and take two big gulps, one after another. As I start to really come around and wake up, I'm struck suddenly by how calm I feel. *Maybe that tablet has worked straight away.* I just lay there listening to Tom and Dad as they kick the ball around in our front garden. *It can't have worked. Not one little tablet, it must be my mind playing tricks on me.*

I stay lying completely still, as if to will the tablet to continue to work its magic, but as soon as I allow my mind to wander I get that all too familiar tingling sensation in my arms. *It doesn't work, that's it, I've had enough, I can't face another minute of this excruciating feeling.* I bang both my arms down in complete frustration hard against my mattress, and I start to well up again, I can't control my tears this time and I bang my face hard against my pillows making sure some of my head will hit my wooden head rest. I want to cause some pain; I need to feel that pain to stop how I'm feeling. *This has got to end; I can't live like this anymore.*

The instant pain I get from hitting my head only slightly eases my anxiety, so I get up and head for the bathroom. I take a look in the mirror and can see that a reddish mark, about the size of an egg has begun to appear on the left side of my forehead. I turn around and lock the door. As soon as I start to run my bath my anticipation begins to grow, it sends an electric excitement throughout my whole body and I start feeling aroused. The anticipation of how I'm going to feel is so overwhelming that I pick up my razor and forcibly make a cut in my right calf whilst still standing up. The blood comes out instantly, so I quickly put one of Pip's wet wipes on the it and try to soak up the blood. I close my eyes and let all that pleasure and pain consume me.

Once I feel the pain and its perverse pleasure start to lessen, I jump into the bath and quickly cut again, this time higher up, but still on the right calf. I keep my eyes open this time and follow the flow of my blood as it trickles down my calf and into the bath water. I continue to watch, totally engrossed by my blood and its flow, finally it starts to slow down and then stops dripping entirely from my skin. So, I begin to wash off the drying blood and take comfort in the control I have over my thoughts and feelings when I can cut out and release all of my pent-up emotions by causing, and controlling, my own pain and pleasure.

I stay lying in the bath and cut myself again. As I do, I hear footsteps coming up the stairs.

"Fran... me and Tom are heading to Eddie's soon, do you want your usual, love?"

"Um... I don't feel that hungry, Dad, to be honest."

"Oh, come on love, it's Friday! What about just some chips then?"

"Um, oh okay, thanks, not too much vinegar on mine, though."

"Okay!... Also, Pam's staying for tea, she's out down the park with Pip at the moment, so she may be back before me and Tom get home, okay? So, I left the front door unlocked, all right?"

"Okay!"

I don't feel hungry at all, but it's just easier to give in then have a long, pointless discussion about it. I stay in my warm bath until I hear Dad and Tom leave for Fat Eddie's. My new cuts feel sore as I step out of the warm bath water, so I dab at them with some toilet paper and grab my towel off the floor. As I begin to dry myself, I try to remember where Dad keeps his toolbox.

It's maybe in our car, or is it in the back porch? I know I've seen it somewhere.

I leave the bathroom and feel completely detached and lost by the time I reach my bedroom.

Dad and Tom will be gone for a least half an hour, and as long as Aunty Pam doesn't come back soon, I'll have enough time to find Dad's toolbox and look for his Stanley knife.

I change back into my earlier clothes and head down the stairs towards the back porch. As I reach the front room all I can picture is my mum; Mum just lying flat out, looking twisted and distorted somehow on our sofa. Taking a deep breath, I walk across our wooden floorboards, they feel cold as I cross them with my bare feet. I reach the glass porch door and can see Dad's toolbox on a shelf at the back of the small room. Again, my feet feel cold as I step onto the bare concrete floor; I reach up and take hold of the toolbox. I nervously look through the glass window back towards the front room and kitchen just to make sure no one has come in. Seeing that it's all empty, I start rifling through Dad's untidy looking plastic toolbox. I find his Stanley knife near the bottom, nestled in between some screwdrivers and an old wooden-handled hammer.

He'll notice his Stanley knife is missing though.

I continue looking, but this time need to find any spare blades. It's taking too long, where are they? Aunty Pam and Pip will be back soon.

Frantically I start pulling things out of the toolbox, until finally I see a small red plastic container. I open it and see four to five brand new Stanley blades loosely wrapped in a small piece of brown paper. I quickly but carefully pick up one of the blades and put it down gently onto the bottom shelf, then I started to put Dad's tools back not caring about what order they go back in.

Closing the porch door behind me, I sprint across the front room and up the stairs. When I reach my bedroom, I lock my door and just sit motionless on my bed.

I can do it, it worked before, I don't need to be in the bath to feel better, this is easier, I can do it whenever I want to.

I start by just lightly scratching the blade against the surface of my skin on my left forearm. At first it just feels like a tickle; I become excited though when I see the small indentation line appear from my first scratch. It seems to take ages before I can make out the thin razor line clearly, but as I do I can see that its becoming red. A few seconds later it begins to bleed.

Shit, I've only really touched the blade against my skin and its cut already.

Fascinated by the sharpness of the blade I try to slowly make a deeper horizontal cut across my left forearm. As the blade pierces my skin, I let out a high-pitched scream of joy, the pain is so intense, and I feel myself become excited and once again start to feel a sense of control. I watch my blood as it oozes out of the clean, precise cut I've just made; it doesn't flow like before but instead seems to explode out of my arm and splatter its bright red spots all over my bed sheets.

Oh my God, this is mental, how does this work? I don't care, it does work, it works for me.

I lie back on my bed now, enjoying the short-lived euphoria I'm feeling. God, what a week this has been. Last Friday I was the happiest I think I've ever been. My first swimming gold medal, what a feeling that was. But just like my short-lived euphoria then, now I've come to be living in this dark, frightening place where my thoughts rule my body and my body and thoughts can only be controlled by self-inflicted pain, and by the sight of my own blood being spilt.

How things have changed in such a short time, my happiest moment shattered by the news of my mum's return home. That overwhelming fear, that utter distress and panic I think and feel when I picture my mum that day, and now she is returning home to the very place that I found her.

Just the idea of seeing Mum in our front room again is so overwhelming, so terrifying that I cut myself again to somehow distract my troubled mind away from my deepest fears. I cut deeper than before, not caring to look as I do so, and when I remove the blade this time, I don't feel any pleasure, I just feel pain, a cry for help that no one can hear, a cry for help that I've decided to keep to myself.

I keep my eyes firmly shut, I don't want to see my own blood this time, so I just lay still, as still as I can. Within my own silence now, I hear our front door opening and can make out the laughter of Tom and Dad; soon after, I hear Aunty Pam's voice as she talks to Pip in the hallway. With all my senses heightened I start to smell that unmistakable smell of our Friday night, that intoxicating smell, the smell of Fat Eddie's and his infamous, finger fat chips and chunky, crispy, battered cod.